The man on the other side of the door took her breath away.

For a moment she forgot all about her anger. Whew!

His Royal Highness, Prince Marc of Broitenburg, dressed in royal regalia, was really something. But just plain Marc, casually dressed in jeans and an open-necked shirt, was something else entirely.

His hair was now ruffled and curled. His gray eyes were smiling, the laughter lines on his tanned face creasing into deep and delicious crinkles. His smile was questioning, and his eyes searched the room until he found the sleeping Henry.

Whew, indeed! He made her want to take a step back.

Or maybe he made her want to take a step forward....

Marion Lennox was born on an Australian dairy farm. She moved on—mostly because the cows weren't interested in her stories! Marion writes Medical Romance™ novels as well as Harlequin Romance® books. Initially she used a different name for each category, so if you're looking for past books, search also for author Trisha David. In her nonwriting life Marion cares (haphazardly) for her husband, teenagers, dogs, cats, chickens and anyone else who lines up at her dinner table. She fights her rampant garden (she's losing) and her house dust (she's lost). She also travels, which she finds seriously addictive. As a teenager Marion was told she'd never get anywhere reading romance. Now romance is the basis of her stories. Her stories allow her to travel, and if ever there was an advertisement for following your dream, she'd be it! You can contact Marion at www.marionlennox.com

Congratulations to Marion Lennox on her 50th book!

Books by Marion Lennox:
HARLEQUIN ROMANCE®

3742—A MILLIONAIRE FOR MOLLY
3726—A ROYAL PROPOSITION

HER ROYAL BABY

Marion Lennox

High Society Brides

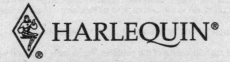

TORONTO • NEW YORK • LONDON
AMSTERDAM • PARIS • SYDNEY • HAMBURG
STOCKHOLM • ATHENS • TOKYO • MILAN • MADRID
PRAGUE • WARSAW • BUDAPEST • AUCKLAND

ISBN 0-373-03784-8

HER ROYAL BABY

First North American Publication 2004.

Copyright © 2003 by Marion Lennox.

Visit us at www.eHarlequin.com

Printed in U.S.A.

CHAPTER ONE

TAMMY was up a tree when royalty arrived.

Royalty might be unusual, but being up a tree wasn't. Tamsin Dexter spent half her life up trees. She was one of Australia's youngest and brightest tree surgeons, and Tammy's passion was propagating, treating or, as a last resort, felling trees and planting new ones to take their place.

Employed by the Australian National Parks Service, Tammy was as usual, working in the remote bushland that she loved so much. She was part of a team, but today she was working happily and successfully alone.

She had nothing to do with royalty.

But someone was under her tree right now and he certainly looked like royalty. Or maybe he was a duke. Or maybe he wasn't royalty. Could he be an admiral or something?

Maybe she didn't know, she conceded. Tammy's working knowledge of royalty, dukes and admirals was strictly limited. Were admirals as young as this? Maybe not.

What the stranger was wearing probably wasn't an admiral's uniform, she decided as she checked him out more closely. He was dressed in a sleek, expensively cut suit, embellished with rows of braid, medals and tassels. He'd arrived in a gleaming limousine, which was now parked under the tree she was working on, and a uniformed chauffeur remained in the driving seat.

Someone else was climbing out of the car now. The second man was older, and wore no braid or medals, but he still looked like some sort of official.

Which of the pair looked more out of place? Tammy

5

couldn't decide. Royalty or official? It didn't matter, but she
knew who looked the most interesting.

Royalty. Definitely royalty.

The man she'd decided was royalty was tall. He was well
over six feet, she thought, though it was tricky to judge from
so far above him. He was immaculately groomed with jet
black hair, thickly waved and raked back. His hair looked
carefully arranged to suit the official status of his uniform,
but perhaps ungroomed it would be the sort of tousled thatch
that Tammy infinitely preferred in her men.

Her men?

She grinned at the direction her thoughts were taking.
That was a laugh. Her men. *Her men* were a figment of her
imagination.

Figment or not, this man looked great. Wonderful. He
was strongly built and had a sort of chiselled look about
him: like one of Rodin's statues. His bone structure was
superb—intensely, wonderfully masculine.

What else? Some things were obvious. He certainly
wasn't the sort who lived in the bush. Even without the
royal regalia, he looked the type who'd be at home drinking
café latte, or sipping wine in trendy city bars, with a sleek
little Lamborghini parked nearby.

She knew the type, and it wasn't her type at all. Cheap
tea boiled on a campfire with a few eucalyptus leaves
thrown in for flavour was more Tammy's style.

So, what on earth were these two men and their chauffeur
doing here? She swung lazily back in her harness and considered.

The bureaucrat was about fifty—twenty years or so older
than the royalty-type—and he was podgy. He was wearing
a dark suit and his shirt had a too-tight collar. In comparison
the younger man looked smooth, intelligent and sophisti-
cated.

What a pair! In combination they looked almost absurd.

Here they were, in the middle of the Australian bush, and they were dressed as if they were expecting a royal reception. And to receive them there was only Tammy, swinging thirty feet above their heads.

What did they want?

'Miss Dexter?' the bureaucrat called, and Tammy frowned. Miss Dexter? That was her. What were this lot doing looking for *her?*

'This is ridiculous,' the royalty guy was saying. 'The sort of woman I'm looking for wouldn't be working in a place like this.'

Tammy thought about that and agreed wholeheartedly. How many Miss Dexters were there in the world? Thousands, she decided. These guys had wandered off a movie set and needed directions to find their way home.

'Miss Dexter?' the bureaucrat called again, this time more urgently.

But still Tammy didn't respond. She stared down at the men below, and as she did she felt her insides give an unfamiliar lurch. Maybe it was a premonition. Maybe they weren't in the wrong place at all.

Maybe they spelled trouble.

'Miss Dexter?' the bureaucrat called again, in a tone that said that this was his last try, and she took a deep breath.

'I'm up here. What can I do for you?'

The voice from above his head made Marc start.

The foreman down the road had told him Tamsin Dexter was working in this clearing and he'd reacted with disbelief. What on earth was one of Lara's family doing working in a place like this? He'd been wondering that pretty much constantly for the last twenty-four hours, when the private investigator he'd hired had told him where he could find her.

'I've found your Tamsin Dexter. She's twenty-seven,

she's single, and she's working as a tree surgeon with the Australian National Parks Service. She's currently working in the National Park behind Bundanoon. Bundanoon's on the Canberra-Sydney Highway, so if you take an hour or so after the Canberra reception you could find her.'

The private investigator had come with excellent credentials, but Marc had reacted with incredulity. How could a tree surgeon be sister to a woman such as Lara? It didn't make sense. It must be the wrong Tamsin Dexter, he'd decided, and he'd sworn in vexation at the potential waste of time. He needed to work fast.

But the government reception in Canberra had been unavoidable. As Broitenburg's Head of State, Marc would step on too many toes if he visited Australia and refused it. So... If he had to attend it wouldn't hurt to detour through Bundanoon and see if he could find the woman.

Now he stared upward, and it was as much as he could do not to gasp out loud.

Tamsin was slim and wiry and...tough, he decided. Or maybe 'serviceable' was the best way to describe her. She was dressed in workmanlike khaki overalls and ancient leather boots. The boots were the closest thing to him, swinging back and forth above his head. They were battered and torn, and the laces had been repaired with knot after knot.

What else? She was young and obviously superbly fit. Her riot of jet-black curls was caught back with a piece of twine. Curls spread out to tangle glossily around her shoulders. They looked as if they hadn't seen a brush for a week. Though that might be unfair. If he was hanging where she was maybe his hair would look tousled as well.

He forced his gaze to move on, assessing the whole package. Her skin was tanned and clear.. weathered, almost. Wide, clear eyes gazed calmly down at him and he found himself wondering what colour they were. Brown, like her sister's? He couldn't tell from here.

But what he could see was a perfect likeness of Lara. Hell, even the similarity made his gut clench in anger.

The detective had been right. This was the Tamsin Dexter he'd been looking for. He'd found her.

'Can I help you?' She was looking down at them as if they were the odd ones out—which, considering their clothes, wasn't surprising. She was still swinging from her harness, reluctant to come down unless it was really necessary.

It was necessary.

'I need you,' he told her.

'Why?'

'You're Tamsin Dexter?'

'Yep.' Still she made no sign of descent. Her attitude said she had work to do and they were interfering with it.

'Miss Dexter, this is His Royal Highness, Marc, Prince Regent of Broitenburg,' Charles interrupted, tugging his collar in anxiety. He wasn't comfortable in this situation and it showed. 'Could you please come down?'

What would the ramifications of being rude to royalty be? The two men watched as she clearly thought about it and decided her best option was to swing a while longer.

'Hi,' she said at last to Marc—the good-looking one— and then she looked across to Charles. The podgy one with the sweaty collar. 'If your friend's a prince, who are you?'

'I'm Charles Debourier. I'm ambassador to—'

'Don't tell me. Let me guess. Ambassador to Broitenburg?'

'Yes.'

'And Broitenburg is…um…somewhere in Europe?' She grinned, a wide, white smile that was so totally different from Lara's careful painted smile that Marc caught his breath at the sight of it.

What was he thinking? She was too much like Lara to interest him, he told himself savagely, and he didn't have time to waste thinking about women. Especially this one.

'You don't know where Broitenburg is?' Charles demanded, and the woman's smile widened. She had a huge advantage over them—thirty feet, in fact.

'I've never been much interested in geography,' she told them. 'And I left school at fifteen.'

Great. She was Lara's sister and illiterate besides. Marc's feelings of dismay intensified.

'Broitenburg's bordered by Austria on one side and Germany on the other,' Charles was saying, but Tammy was clearly unimpressed.

'Oh, right. Come to think of it, I have heard of it. It's small, huh?'

'It's an important country in its own right,' Charles snapped.

'I guess it must be, to send an ambassador to Australia.' She grinned again. 'Well, it was nice to met you, Your Highness and Your Ambassadorship, and it was good of you to drop by, but I have a job to do before dusk.'

'I told you,' Marc said stiffly. 'I need you.'

She'd been preparing to climb again, but she stopped at that. 'Why? Do you have trees in Broitenburg?'

'Yes, but...'

'I'm not interested in job offers.'

She sounded as if she was serious, Marc thought incredulously. She sounded as if she seriously thought he'd travelled all the way to Australia and come to find her in this outlandish place, dressed in this ridiculous rig, *to ask her to look after some trees*?

He hated it. He hated this ornate, over-the-top uniform. He hated Charles's damned ostentatious car and his chauffeur. He hated royalty.

And the only way to get rid of it was via this chit of a girl.

'I'm not offering you a job,' he told her stiffly, and she stared.

'Then why…?'

'I'm here to ask you to sign some release papers,' Marc told her. 'So I can take your nephew back to Broitenburg where he belongs.'

Silence.

The silence went on for so long that it became clear there was lots going on behind it. This was no void, for want of anything to say. This was a respite, where all could get their heads around what had been said.

Tammy had hauled herself up onto a branch and now she sat stock still, staring down as Marc stared back up at her.

She was accustomed to people hunting for her with job offers—which was crazy, as she didn't intend to leave Australia ever again—but this was crazier still.

Charles discovered there were ants crawling over one of his shoes, and started shifting from foot to foot. He glanced up at Tammy and then at Marc before returning his gaze to the ants. Annoyed, or maybe to block out the silence, he started stomping on them.

His action gave Tammy more breathing space. 'Excuse me, but those ants are protected,' Tammy said at last, almost conversationally, as though the previous words had not been said at all. 'You're in a National Park. The ants here have more rights than you do.'

Charles swore and shifted sideways. Onto more ants. He swore again, and cast an uncertain glance at Marc, and then, when Marc didn't speak, he shrugged and headed for the car. He'd done his job. He hadn't taken on an ambassador-ship to stand under trees being bitten by ants.

'I said, I want to take your nephew—' Marc said at last, and Tammy interrupted.

'I know what you said. But I don't know what you're talking about.'

Marc nodded. He'd expected as much. There'd been no wish to come to her sister's funeral. There'd been no contact made with the child. If it wasn't for the immigration authorities he could pick the little boy up and take him back to his country right now. She probably didn't even admit responsibility for him. At the thought of Henry's neglect, he felt his face darken with anger.

'If you'd been in contact they would have told you I'd requested he be returned, but they need your consent.'

'Um…' She was regarding him as if he was slightly off balance. 'Who are *they?*'

'The child's nanny and the immigration authorities,' he snapped, and now he could control himself no longer. 'You can't object. You've shown yourself to be the world's worst custodian. If I hadn't been paying the nanny's salary he'd be in foster care right now. You and your sister and your mother…you should be locked up, the three of you. Of all the uncaring—'

He caught himself. Anger would achieve nothing, he told himself grimly. This woman didn't want the child. It was enough that she signed the papers and he could be done with the entire mess. 'I'm sorry,' he said stiffly. 'But your sister's dead, your mother doesn't give a damn, and apparently neither do you. All I want is the release papers. You sign them for me, I'll take Henry back to Broitenburg, and you'll never see him again.'

Her look of confusion was absolute. 'Henry?'

Hadn't she even bothered to remember the little boy's name? Marc thought back to the bereft little boy he'd left in Sydney and felt his anger rising all over again.

'Your nephew.'

'I don't have a nephew.'

That took him aback. He stared up at her. 'Of course you do.'

'There's no *of course* about it. You must have mistaken me for someone else. I only have one sister—Lara—who I haven't seen for years. That's the way we like it. Last time I saw Lara she was attached to a millionaire up on the Gold Coast, and if you're asking me if she has children I'd say you'd have to be joking. Lara would no sooner risk losing her gorgeous figure through childbearing than she would fly. Now, if you don't mind...'

It was absurd, Marc thought. The whole scenario was absurd. She was lifting a drill and any minute now she'd turn it on, drowning out his words with her noise.

But she'd said her sister's name. Lara. It confirmed what he had already been sure of. This woman was Lara's sister.

But what had she said? She hadn't seen her for years? The anger faded. Dear God, then she didn't know.

'Lara Dexter was your sister?'

'Is,' she snapped, and he heard the sudden surge of fear behind her irritation.

He took a deep breath. He hadn't expected this. What the hell was the mother playing at? If she really hadn't been told... He stared up at the girl in the tree and thought, where on earth did he go from here?

There was nowhere to go but forward. There was no easy way to say what had to be said.

'Miss Dexter, I'm sorry, but your sister was married to my cousin. They were married three years ago. Jean-Paul and Lara were killed at a ski resort in Italy five weeks back. They have a child, Henry, who's currently living in Sydney. He's being cared for by a nanny whose wages I've been paying, but his care...his care is less than satisfactory. He's ten months old. I'm here to ask your permission to take him back to Broitenburg.'

* * *

Tammy's world stopped right there.

She froze. The drill in her hands seemed suddenly a stupid thing to be holding, and she stared at it as if she didn't know what it was.

She had a makeshift bench set up on the branch she was sitting on. Carefully she laid the drill down and stared at it some more.

Lara was…dead?

'I don't believe you,' she whispered, still not looking at the man below. She was concentrating on the drill, as if working out its function was the most important thing in the world. There was a part of her that didn't want to move forward from this moment.

Thirty seconds ago this stranger hadn't said any of this. That was where she wanted to be. Back in time.

Lara…*dead?*

'I'm sorry,' he said, and something inside her snapped.

'I'm sorry too,' she flung at him. 'I'm sorry about this whole damned mess. I don't believe any of it. You come here, in your outlandish, stupid costume, like you're a king or something—which I don't believe—with your stupid chauffeured car and your tame politician, and you stomp my ants and interfere with my work and tell me Lara is dead…'

'Lara *is* dead.'

'I don't believe it.'

'Will you come down?'

'No.' She made to pick the drill up again, but his voice cut through her confusion and her rage.

'Miss Dexter, you need to face this. Your sister is dead. Will you come down from the tree, please?'

She flinched—and she thought about it.

For about three minutes she simply sat on her branch and stared down at him. He stared back, his face calm and compassionate.

It was a good face, she thought inconsequentially, and maybe that was another way of avoiding acceptance of what he'd just said. Kind. Strong. Determined. His eyes were calm and sure, promising that he spoke the truth.

She could accept or reject what he was telling her. His eyes said that the truth was here for the taking.

The minutes ticked on, and he had the sense to let her alone. To allow her time to believe. His face stayed impassive.

His eyes never wavered.

And finally she faced the inevitable. She believed him, she decided at last. Dreadfully, she believed him. Despite the incongruity of the situation—despite the craziness of what he was wearing and what he was saying—what he was telling her was the truth.

And with that knowledge came the first ghastly wash of pain. Her little sister...

Lara had wanted nothing to do with her for years. Lara and their mother lived in a world of their own that Tammy had nothing to do with, but for the first years of Lara's life it had been Tammy who'd cared, who'd acted as a surrogate mother as far as a child could, because their own mother hadn't known what was involved in the job of mothering. Before Lara was born Tammy had nothing. When Lara had become old enough to join forces with their mother she had nothing again. But for that short sweet while...

Lara was five years younger than Tammy. Twenty-two.

Lara was dead?

A vision of the little girl she'd loved and cuddled through her childhood lurched into her mind, and with it came a pain that was well nigh unbearable. The colour washed from her face and she put a hand on her branch to steady herself.

'Come down,' Marc said strongly, and Tammy took a deep breath and came to a decision. There was no going back. She had to face it.

She swung her legs over the branch, adjusted the harness and slid down.

She came down too fast.

Tammy had been abseiling up and down trees since she was a child. She could do it in her sleep. But now... She was almost past thinking and her hands slipped as she adjusted the rope. She came down faster than she should have—not fast enough to hurt herself, but fast enough for Marc to step in urgently to catch her, to steady her and to take her weight as she hit the ground.

Which left her standing right against him, his hands on her shoulders to balance her, her slight body being supported by his stronger one.

Strong...

Strong described him absolutely, she thought. His whole body was rock-solid. Tammy was five feet six and slightly built, diminutive in the presence of this much larger man. He'd caught her and held her without apparent effort, and now he was staring down at her with the first trace of concern in his face.

'Are you okay?'

She thought about it. Okay? Okay was a long way from how she felt right now. His hands were gripping her shoulders and she had an almost overpowering compulsion to place her face on his chest and burst into tears.

No. She hadn't cried for as long as she could remember and she wasn't about to start now.

'I'm fine.' But her voice wobbled.

'You truly didn't know your sister was dead?'

She concentrated fiercely on the row of medals pinned to his chest. She even counted them. Six. The fabric of his suit was a fine worsted wool, she thought. Nice. She could bury her face in his chest—hide from the pain that was threatening to overwhelm her.

'You didn't know?' he said gently as he put her away

from him, still holding her but forcing her to look up at him. His fingers were under her chin, cupping her face to meet his eyes.

A girl could drown in those eyes. A girl might want to. Anything but face this scorching, ghastly pain.

'I…my sister and I have been…apart for ever,' she whispered. 'We don't…'

'I see.' He didn't. His voice said he was totally confused, and Tammy made a Herculean effort to make her voice work.

'My sister and I didn't get on.'

'I'm sorry.'

'Don't be.' She let herself stay motionless for one more long moment, as if drawing strength from the warmth and size of him. Then she hauled herself bleakly together and pulled away. He released her, but the way he did it was curious. It was almost as if he was reluctant to let her go.

Questions. She had to ask questions. She needed to know—but she didn't want to.

She must.

'You said…she died in a skiing accident?'

'Yes.' His face was still calm. She was standing two feet back from him, gazing up into his eyes as if trying to read him. Trying to find some sort of comfort in his calmness.

'H…how?'

'They took out a bobsled.' His face tightened for a minute, as if in anger. 'They took it on a black run—a run for experienced skiers only. Bobsledding in those conditions is madness. I'm afraid…I'm afraid they'd been drinking.'

The knot of pain in Tammy's stomach tightened. Oh, you fool, she thought bleakly. Lara, you fool. It took an almost overpowering effort of will to go on. 'So…' It was so hard to speak. It was as if her voice didn't belong to her. 'She…Lara was married to your cousin?'

'Yes.'

'And your cousin died, too?'

'Jean-Paul died, yes.'

She couldn't see what he was thinking. His face was still impassive. Was there pain there? She couldn't tell.

'I'm sorry.'

'I guess we're both sorry.'

He had a nice voice, she thought dispassionately. Deep and rumbly. It was tinged with what sounded almost like a French accent, but it was very slight. He'd been well schooled in English.

She wasn't supposed to be thinking about this man's voice. Or maybe she was still using thoughts to distract herself.

Lara was dead.

What else had he said? They had a baby?

'I can't believe that you don't know about this.' Marc's voice was suddenly rough, tinged again with anger. 'That your mother didn't tell you.'

'My mother knows?'

'Of course your mother knows. I flew her to Broitenburg for the funeral. They were buried with a State funeral last month.'

Her mother would have enjoyed that, Tammy thought inconsequentially, going off on another tangent as her mind darted back and forth, trying to avoid pain. She thought of Isobelle Dexter de Bier as a grieving mother at a royal funeral. Isobelle would have done it brilliantly. She could almost guess what her mother would have worn. It would have been something lacy and black and extremely elegant. She'd have worn a veil, and there'd have been a wispy handkerchief dabbing at eyes that welled with tears that were never allowed to fall.

'Was...was she alone?'

'Your stepfather came with her.'

Oh, of course. Which stepfather was this? Tammy bit her

lip, anger welling. Isobelle didn't bother to marry her lovers any more, which was just as well. Tammy's mother had been up to husband number four when Lara was born.

Lara was dead?

Lara was buried.

And there'd been a funeral. She should have been there, she thought bleakly. She should have been there as she'd been there for Lara since birth. Of all the things her mother had done to her, maybe this was the worst. To bury Lara with only her mother...

'You were fond of your sister?' Marc didn't understand. He was staring at her with the same confusion she was feeling—maybe even more so.

'Once,' she said brusquely. 'A long time ago.'

'You've completely lost contact?'

'Yes.'

'And with your mother?'

'Do you think my mother would admit she has a daughter who was a tree surgeon? That she has a daughter who looks like *this*?'

His calm gaze raked her from the toes up, but his face stayed impassive and his voice stayed gravely calm. She couldn't tell what he was thinking. 'I can't say,' he told her. 'Maybe not.'

Maybe definitely. 'Look, I think I need time to take this in.' She was glaring at him now. Maybe her anger was misdirected, but she needed space to come to terms with what she'd learned. 'Have you got a card or something to tell me where I can contact you? I need...'

She hesitated, but she knew what she needed. To be alone. She'd learned early that solitude was the only solution to pain. It didn't stop anything, but alone she could haul her features back into control, adjust the mask and get herself ready to face the world again. 'Can you just leave me be? Contact me tomorrow if you must. But for now...'

'I'm sorry, but I can't do that.'

'Why not?'

'I need to be back in Sydney tonight, and then I'm leaving for Broitenburg immediately,' Marc told her. 'I've brought the release papers with me. You need to sign them. Then I'll take Henry back to Broitenburg and let you have all the solitude you want.'

CHAPTER TWO

HE HADN'T expected this. Marc hadn't known what to expect of Lara's sister but it certainly wasn't the woman standing before him.

She looked bereft, he thought, and he accepted that she really hadn't known about her sister's death. Which led him to Isobelle. Their mother.

What sort of mother would not tell one daughter about another's death?

It wasn't any of his business, he told himself savagely. His job was to get the papers signed and get out of here. Heaven knew a trip to Australia at this time was a luxury he couldn't afford. Jean-Paul's death had left a huge mess at home. He needed to collect the child and go.

He just needed the signature, but, judging by the look of devastation on the face of the girl before him, it was going to be tricky.

Maybe he could just push the papers in front of her and say *sign*. Maybe she would. She looked so shocked he could push her right over and she wouldn't fight back.

He shouldn't do it—he should give her time—but it was his country he was fighting for. Henry's country. Henry's inheritance.

And his own freedom.

'I need you to sign,' he repeated, this time more gently, and he motioned to the car. 'I have the papers here.'

'What papers?'

'The release papers.'

'I still don't understand what you're talking about.' She was standing as if she'd been turned to stone. Her face was

21

totally devoid of colour and he thought she looked as if she was about to topple over. She looked sick.

He made an involuntary gesture of comfort, holding out a hand—and then he pulled it away. What was he thinking of? He needed as little contact here as possible. He couldn't possibly comfort this woman.

'I need the release papers to allow me to take Henry back to Broitenburg.'

She thought about that. 'Lara did have a child?'

'Yes.'

'I didn't know.' She looked up at him, her eyes bleak with shock. 'I didn't know anything about a baby.' It was a despairing wail. 'Surely if she'd had a child she would have contacted me. If she was in trouble…'

'Your sister wasn't in trouble,' Marc told her. 'She married Jean-Paul and she had everything she'd ever wanted. A royal marriage. Servants. Luxury you can't begin to imagine.'

'She never would have wanted a child.'

Marc nodded. That fitted with what he knew of Lara, but there was an explanation. 'Jean-Paul needed an heir,' he told her. 'He was Crown Prince of Broitenburg. He wouldn't have married Lara if she hadn't been prepared to give him a child.'

Tammy thought about that, too, and it almost made sense. Maybe with Lara's warped sense of values marrying royalty would be worth the cost of having a child. She knew her mother and Lara so well. She knew the way they thought. Money and status were everything. For Lara to be a royal bride… Yes. It was a price Lara might well have been prepared to pay.

'So she had a child? Henry?'

'Yes.'

'But you said Henry was here. In Australia. In Sydney.'

'Lara sent him back to Australia about four months ago.'

'Why?'

'Does it matter?'

'Yes, it does matter.' Anger and sadness were surging back and forth, and now anger won. 'You tell me my sister married and had a baby, and was royal, and is now dead. You tell me you want the baby. And when I ask questions you say ''Does it matter?''' Her eyes narrowed. 'Why are you here? Obviously my mother didn't think it was worth telling me of my sister's death. And my sister didn't bother to tell me of her marriage or the birth of her child. So why are you here now? What are you demanding that I sign? What does all this have to do with me?'

Marc took a deep breath. He didn't want this. He just needed a signature and then he'd leave. He had enough complications without this, and, looking at her face, he knew a complication was looming right now.

'Your sister named you as Henry's legal guardian in the event of her death,' he told her. 'If Henry was still in Broitenburg it wouldn't matter, but because he's here your Department of Foreign Affairs say I can't take him out of Australia without your permission.'

It was all too much. Tammy stared at Marc for a long, long moment and then silently slipped her harness from her shoulders. She lifted a radio handset from her belt.

She didn't look at Marc.

'Doug?' she said into the radio, and Marc thought back to the foreman he'd met down the road, organising the rest of the team—two young women and an older man. That'd be Doug, then. 'The people in the big car who were looking for me?' she was saying. 'They've told me that my sister and her husband have been killed and their baby—my nephew—is alone in Sydney. Can I leave my gear here and have you pick it up? I'm going to Sydney and I need to leave now.'

There was a crackle of static, and then a man's voice raised in concern.

'Yeah, I know it's the pits,' Tammy said bleakly. 'But I've got to go, Doug. No, I don't know how long I'll be away. As long as it takes. Put Lucy onto the tree I'm working on now. She has the skills. But for now... I'll be in touch.'

Then she laid the handset on the ground with her harness. She lifted a backpack that was lying nearby and heaved it over her shoulder. It was an action that spoke of decision.

'You're going back to Sydney now?' she asked, still with that curious detachment.

'Yes, but—'

'But nothing,' she told him. 'Take me with you.'

'Take you to Sydney?'

'Yes.'

'Why?'

'It's obvious, isn't it?' she snapped. 'You tell me I have a nephew and I'm his guardian—'

'He doesn't need you.'

That was blunt. She paused and bit her lip. 'So he has someone who loves him?' she demanded, and it was his turn to pause.

'He has people—a nanny who's caring for him—and once I have him back to Broitenburg I'll employ someone thoroughly competent.'

Competent. The word hung between both of them and Marc immediately knew that it wasn't enough.

'That's not what I asked,' she said.

He knew what she meant but was helpless to offer more. 'I...'

'Why on earth did Lara send him home?'

'I don't know,' he admitted honestly. 'It seemed odd to me. But Jean-Paul and Lara were in Paris four months ago. Then they were in Italy and Switzerland. I've seen neither of them since just after the child was born. It wasn't until after their death that I knew the child had been sent to Australia.'

The child...

That was a mistake. The brief description was chilling, even to him, and it made everything suddenly worse. Bleaker. Marc thought about it and amended it. 'Henry,' he said gently, and Tammy flushed.

'Yeah. Henry. *The child.* How old did you say he is?'

'Ten months.'

'And he's heir to some royal thing?'

'Yes.'

'And so you want to take him back to Broitenburg so he can be looked after by nannies in the lap of luxury until he's old enough to be king?'

'Prince,' Marc corrected her. 'Broitenburg is a principality.'

'Prince, then. Whatever,' she said distractedly. 'It makes no difference. Are you married?'

'What?'

'You heard. Are you married?'

'No. I...'

'So who gets to play mother to Henry?'

'I told you. He'll have nannies. The best.'

'But as legal guardian I get to decide whether he goes or not.'

She'd cornered him. He hadn't wanted to admit it. Get her signature and get the child. At home it had seemed easy.

'If you refuse to let him return to Broitenburg I'll apply for custody myself,' he said stiffly.

'You do that. You're going home tomorrow, did you say? Good luck getting legal custody by then.'

He took a deep breath, trying to control his temper. There'd been no one near the child for months and now this! 'Until five minutes ago you didn't know of the child's existence. You can't want him.'

'So why do *you* want him?'

'He's part of the Broitenburg royal family. A very important part. He has to come home.'

'But maybe he's my family, too,' Tammy muttered. She swung open the front passenger door of the limousine and tossed her pack on the floor. Then she climbed in after it, sat down against the luxurious leather and stared straight ahead, refusing to look back at Marc. 'Maybe he needs me. As I see it, it's up to me to decide. So, are you going to take me to Sydney or are you planning on making me catch a bus? Either way, I'm signing nothing until I've seen him— and maybe not even then.'

It was an incredibly strained journey.

How could she just pick up her pack and leave? Marc wondered. Most women—all the women he'd ever met— would have taken hours to prepare. Hours to decide. But Tammy appeared to have everything she needed in the battered pack at her feet and wanted nothing else.

'I have a tent, a sleeping bag, a toothbrush and enough food and water for twenty-four hours,' she told him when he enquired how she could just leave her work and make the journey to Sydney without further fuss. 'We were planning to camp out tonight.'

'So now you're planning on camping somewhere in Sydney's parks?' he asked, and she glowered, and went right on staring straight ahead.

'I'll get a hotel. You needn't worry about me. Just show me where my nephew is and I'll look after myself. I'm not asking any favours from you.'

He was right up there with all the people who'd failed to tell her of her sister's death and the existence of her nephew, he thought grimly. Her loathing sounded clearly through the tight-clenched words. He was useful as a tool for getting her to see her nephew—nothing more.

So how the hell was he to get her to sign release papers?

It'd have to be money, he thought, as he sat back beside Charles and the big car nosed its way towards Sydney. She looked as if she didn't have a penny to spare. Her sister had married for money. Money would no doubt buy Henry for him.

He had to play it right, though. He had to give her time to settle. If he offered money right at this minute she might throw it back at him just to spite him.

No. Let her see the baby—tell her how much it cost to pay for decent childcare—give her time to realise how impossible it was for her to keep the child in Australia...

Could he do that in one night?

He must, he thought. *He must.*

He had to get home! The problems Jean-Paul had left were massive. If he wasn't careful the entire monarchy would crumble. That would be okay if there was a decent government to take its place, but Jean-Paul had been running the country like a miniature despot for years, milking it for every penny he could. He'd manipulated the parliament so that politicians were paid peanuts, and if you paid peanuts you got monkeys. There had to be major political reform, and the only way to do that was to ensure the continuity of the royal line.

Which meant getting Henry home.

But it was so complicated. He hadn't realised Lara had registered Henry's birth in Australia. He hadn't thought Lara would have had so much gumption. The knowledge had shocked him. But Henry now held dual citizenship. The Australian authorities wouldn't let him leave without Tammy's say-so, so what was supposed to have been a flying visit to collect his small relative was turning into a nightmare.

'Tell me who's looking after him?' Tammy asked from the front seat, and he had to force himself to think about his response.

'A nanny.'

'I know what she is. Tell me about her.'

'I'm sorry, but...'

'You don't know?'

'She's an Australian girl,' Marc said reluctantly, knowing that what he was saying wouldn't reflect well on any of them. 'I employed her through an agency after the woman who came here with your mother left.'

'My mother!'

'Lara sent Henry back here when your mother last visited her. I gather your mother saw them in Paris, when Henry was about six months old. When your mother came back to Australia Lara asked her to bring Henry with her.'

'My mother...' Tammy swung around to stare at him in incredulity. 'My mother would never agree to look after a baby.'

'No.' They agreed about that. Marc thought about what he knew of Isobelle and his lip curled in contempt. 'Henry came with a nanny from Broitenburg. Your mother installed them in an expensive hotel in Sydney—which Lara was supposed to pay for—and left them. Then it seems the nanny wasn't paid. She'd been given a return flight to Broitenburg, so she left. The first I heard of it was last week. Your mother had assured me at the funeral that Henry was being cared for in Australia, and I assumed...I assumed he was with your family. The assumption was stupid. The next thing I heard was a message from your department of Social Services to say Henry had been abandoned. I managed to employ an Australian nanny through an agency here, set them back up in a hotel, and came as soon as I could.'

There was a sharp intake of angry breath, and then more silence.

What was she thinking? Marc thought, but he knew what he'd be thinking if it was him receiving this news. He knew what he had thought when he'd received the phone call from Australia saying Henry had been abandoned.

He'd been stunned.

He'd known Isobelle had taken the little boy back to Australia, and he'd assumed that she'd had his care in hand. But his phone call to Lara's mother had elicited exactly nothing.

'The child's arrangements have nothing to do with me,' Isobelle had told him when he'd finally tracked her down. She was somewhere in Texas with her latest man, recovering miraculously from her daughter's death and obviously far too busy to be concerned with her grandson's welfare. 'Yes, the child and the nanny Lara employed came back with me four months ago, and I last saw them in Sydney. I assumed Jean-Paul and Lara had left the girl well provided for. It's no fault of mine if the wretched girl's done a bunk.'

Marc had stood by the phone and had willed—ached— for his cousin to still be alive so he could wring his selfish neck. Then he'd set about doing everything to shore up the country's political stability before he'd come to find his cousin's baby son. Heir to the throne.

And he'd found this.

'He'll be well looked after from now on,' he said angrily, his fury matching that emanating from the front passenger seat. From Tammy. 'I promise.'

'I know he will be,' Tammy muttered, but she was speaking to herself. Not to him.

The hotel Henry and his nanny were staying in was one of Sydney's finest, on the Rocks in Sydney Harbour. The limousine nosed into the driveway, a uniformed concierge bowed and opened the door to Marc, then looked askance as Tammy climbed out, too.

There was a plush red carpet leading to the magnificent glass entry. A waterfall fell on either side of the doorway over carefully landscaped rocks. Inside the wide glass doors Tammy could see chandeliers and a vast grand piano. The strains of Chopin were wafting out over the sound of the gently tinkling water.

This was where Marc had installed Henry and his nanny? Money clearly wasn't an issue with His Highness, Prince Marc.

But she didn't intend to be intimidated. Tammy dumped her pack on the red carpet, wiped a little dust from her overalls and looked about her with every appearance of nonchalance.

'Will you be all right?' Charles had emerged from the car and was looking at Marc with some anxiety. He seemed to think Tammy might somehow contaminate Marc. 'You don't wish to stay at the embassy tonight, Your Highness?'

'I'll be fine here.' Marc glanced at his watch. 'If you could collect me and the boy at eleven tomorrow…? The flight is at two.'

'I'll do that.' With a last worried glance at Tammy, Charles disappeared back into the limo—which left Marc and Tammy standing on the red carpet together.

A prince with his princess? Tammy looked Marc up and down, then glanced down at her worn boots and almost smiled.

Almost. Smiling was actually a long way from what she felt like doing.

'Take me to Henry.'

'You don't want to clean up first?'

She glared at him then. Really glared. 'How old did you tell me Henry was?'

'Ten months.'

'You think he's going to judge me because of a little dirt?'

'I…no.'

'So what's the problem?'

The concierge was still hovering, holding the door for them to enter, but by his expression Tammy could tell that given half a hint he'd grab her and haul her away. She looked the type who'd be annoying the customers, not paying to be here.

'It's all right,' she told him. 'I'm not about to mug His Royal Highness. I just want to see my nephew.' She heaved her pack up over her shoulder and stomped through into the plush foyer, leaving Marc to follow.

Marc stared after her for a long moment—and then shrugged and followed.

The suite Henry and his nanny were occupying was on the sixth floor. Marc knocked once, knocked again, and the door finally swung wide.

Most people's first instinct would be to glance at the view—from this position it was spectacular—but Sydney's Opera House and the Harbour Bridge beyond held no interest for Tammy. Her eyes were all on Henry. She brushed past Marc and was in the room before he was.

He was just like Lara!

Lara had been the loveliest baby. Tammy's sister had been born with a fuzz of dark curls and huge brown eyes that had seemed to take over her entire face. She'd had a smile that could light up a room.

And here was Henry, and Henry was just the same. The only difference was that this little boy wasn't smiling. He was seated in his cot beside the window, watching the harbour below. His eyes were wide and wary, but there was no trace of the smile his mother seemed to have been born with. As Tammy and Marc came through the door he turned to see who was entering his world, but there was no hint of expectation in his eyes.

He looked like a child who had no one.

The nanny had been reading, Tammy saw. A paperback had been hastily thrust aside and a daytime television programme was blaring. The little boy was wide awake but he was simply sitting in his cot. There wasn't a toy in sight. His only distraction was the window.

And the nanny had been watching television and reading. Dear heaven…

Tammy dropped her pack and was across the room in seconds, gathering the little boy into her arms as if he was her own. As her face nestled into the familiar curls, as she smelled the familiar scent of baby powder and…well, just baby…it was all too much. Until this minute what Marc was telling her had been a fairy tale. But this was real. Henry was real.

For the first time in years she burst into tears.

The child didn't respond. He held himself stiffly against her, his small body rigid. His expression didn't change at all.

Slowly Tammy pulled herself together. She was aware that the other adults were watching her without comment— the nanny, who looked about sixteen, and Marc. Their expressions were wary, as if they didn't know where they'd go from here.

Which was maybe just as well, as Tammy didn't know where she was going either.

There was a vast armchair beside her. She sank into it, perching Henry on her lap so she could look at him properly.

The little boy gazed back up at her, and then his gaze returned to the window. Windows were more important than people, his expression said.

'Henry?' It was a faint whisper against his cheek, but the child didn't respond.

'He doesn't answer to his name,' the nanny said, as

if it was something Tammy should know. 'He's only ten months old.'

That didn't make sense. 'He's sitting up,' Tammy said. He'd been sitting in his cot as they entered. 'Is he crawling?'

'Yeah.'

'Then surely he should know his name. If he's crawling that means he's developing fine.'

'I guess,' the nanny said indifferently. 'He's pretty advanced.'

'But he still doesn't respond. Does he say anything?'

'No. Why should he?'

Why should he indeed? The little boy's stare was lacklustre, as if he was bored with what was before him. Maybe if Tammy had been staring at the same view for weeks on end…

'Do you play with him?' Tammy asked, and watched as the girl cast a furtive glance at her novel.

'Of course I do.'

'Of course nothing.' Her fury was mounting, until she felt like hitting out. She was hugging the little boy to her, and that stopped her raising her voice, but her fury was barely disguised in her whisper. 'This isn't normal.'

'I'll get him a proper full-time nanny when we return to Broitenburg,' Marc told her, and Tammy could hear the uneasiness in his own voice. He knew what the problem was. 'Kylie was employed via an agency and the situation was urgent. I was lucky to get her at short notice.'

'So he's been with Kylie, or someone like her, since his parents died?' Tammy was stroking the little boy's curls, trying to find some sort of response from him. 'Or longer. Has he been with nannies since birth?'

'I'd imagine so,' Marc told her. 'I don't know.'

'Does anyone know?' She rose then, standing to her full five feet six inches and glaring at the pair of them. She held the baby against her as if she was prepared to battle the world on his behalf. 'Does anyone know anything about how my nephew has been cared for? He's obviously been fed and clothed. Has anything else been done?'

'I...'

'Anything at all?' Tammy's rage was threatening to overwhelm her. 'Have you ever seen anyone give this little boy a hug? Has anyone ever played peek-a-boo with him? Has anyone *loved him*?'

Marc bit his lip. He was on the back foot here, and he knew it. 'He'll be looked after when he gets home.'

'No,' she snapped. 'Or at least not by you he won't. Nor any of your nannies—even if you have nannies by the thousand. If Lara's named me legal guardian then I can only be thankful. Henry's at home right now. He's staying in Australia and he's staying with me. Thank you very much for bringing his situation to my attention, Prince Whatever-Your-Name-Is, but I don't think we need trouble you further. If I can just collect his things, I'll take him now.'

'But—'

'I'm his legal guardian. The rest of you can go to hell!'

CHAPTER THREE

SHE wasn't budging.

Tammy didn't release the child for a moment, almost as if she feared if she put him down Marc would snatch him from her. She held him tight and moved around the room, collecting anything that looked like his and tossing it into a heap on the armchair.

'Can we talk about this?' Marc demanded and Tammy shook her head.

'There's nothing to talk about.'

'You can't take him.'

'Watch me.'

'You can't afford to keep him.'

That stopped her. She whirled to face him, her face rigid with fury. 'No,' she snapped. 'I can't afford to keep him—like this.' She motioned around her at the five-star luxury and the glorious views. 'But if you think this is what he needs then you're mistaken. He doesn't need money. He doesn't need nannies and views and Room Service. He needs hugs and cuddles and someone who cares. Which you've shown very clearly that you don't.'

'I do.'

'Yeah. Pull the other leg. It plays "Jingle Bells".'

'Will you slow down?' She was tossing a packet of milk formula onto her pile with such ferocity that it bounced onto the floor.

'No.'

'Please?'

'*No!*'

35

'Have you thought it through? How can you look after a baby?'

'I can look after a baby better than you.'

'You obviously don't have the money for decent child-care.'

'Who says I don't?' Another formula packet hit the first and suffered a similar fate. Marc leaned over and retrieved both packets, setting them side by side on the chair. Behind them the nanny—Kylie—looked on with wide-eyed wonder.

'You don't have spare money. I just need to look at you to tell…'

Mistake. Bad tactical error. There was one packet of formula open. Tammy lifted it up, stared at it—and then threw it straight at Marc.

It sprayed out in all directions, covering him with a white misting powder. The parcel hit him mid-chest, and slowly slid to the floor.

The action shocked them all. Tammy stopped dead and stared at the white-dusted man before her—and then she winced.

'I'm sorry,' she said at last. 'I shouldn't have done that.'

'It's my best uniform,' he told her, but was that a slight quiver in his face? Surely not. Surely he couldn't be close to laughter. And why did she suddenly feel she was fighting back the same emotion?

'I guess you have hundreds more at home,' she managed, and he nodded.

'Yeah, but they're at home.'

'Gee, you're going to have to travel home like that, then.'

'I do have other clothes.'

'Brocade and velvet and the odd crown and stuff?' she agreed.

'I'm not always dressed up in this rig.'

'Bully for you.' She purposefully turned her attention away from his powder-coated form—and the sudden and unexpected gleam of laughter in his dark eyes—and concentrated on her pile again. Fiercely. 'Do you have anything I can put these things in?'

'I have no idea.' He was watching her, fascinated. 'Kylie, do we have anything we can put these things in?'

'I dunno,' Kylie said resentfully. The nanny was looking more confused by the minute. 'If she's taking the kid, does that mean you don't want me any more?'

'His aunt has authority to care for him. I'll pay you to the end of the month,' Marc told her, and her face cleared.

'All right, then. I'm fed up with this job anyway.' She beamed at Tammy as if she was releasing her from a life sentence and began to be helpful. 'There's suitcases in his bedroom. You're not his Aunty Tammy, are you?'

Tammy paused. 'Yes.' She focused on the girl—sort of. It was actually really hard not to stay focusing on Marc. The dangerous gleam was still in Marc's eyes. He might look ridiculous—a prince with powder coating—but he still packed a lethal punch. Big and handsome and magnetically attractive...

But she needed to concentrate on what the nanny was saying. 'You knew about me?' she managed.

'There's this letter addressed to you. It's in one of the suitcases.

'A letter? From who?'

'I dunno,' Kylie said. 'I saw it when I packed away the baby stuff he'd grown out of. It's addressed to a Tamsin Dexter and underneath is written ''Aunty Tammy''—in quotation marks, like the title's a bit of a joke. There's no address or I would have posted it.'

'Fetch it,' Marc told her, his eyes resting on Tammy. He was clutching at straws now. This might buy him some time. Somehow he needed a way of talking this woman into seeing reason, and it was growing less possible by the minute.

Tammy's anger was still firing her actions, and the worst

part of it was that her anger was reasonable. Henry's treatment made him furious himself.

'Sure.' Kylie cast an uncertain glance at the pair of them and flounced out of the room.

'Fetch the whole suitcase,' Tammy called after her. 'I need to pack this stuff.'

'Okay.' But the girl's voice was muffled. She was already foraging in what must be enormous storage cupboards. This was some hotel.

Marc and Tammy were left glaring at each other, the only thing between them one little boy. Henry gazed back and forth between this unlikely pair of adults, his face showing no emotion at all.

'You can't just take him,' Marc said conversationally and Tammy raised her eyebrows in polite disagreement.

'Yes, I can. You said he's an Australian citizen and I'm his aunt. And his guardian. You're not even his uncle.'

'No, but—'

'But nothing. Blood counts.'

'Your mother has given me permission,' he told her, but even he knew he was clutching at straws. The more he saw of Tammy the more he realised that she was intelligent, and she discarded his statement before he could finish saying it.

'My mother would promise anything if money was involved. If Lara made a will naming me Henry's guardian, surely that's what matters?'

Marc took a deep breath, fighting for words. 'Look, Miss…'

'Tammy,' Tammy said pleasantly—and waited.

'Tammy. Can we at least discuss this?'

'That's what I'm doing.'

'You've already made up your mind.'

'To care for my nephew? Yes, I have. I don't have a choice because I don't see that anyone else is doing it.'

'I promise you—he'll be looked after in Broitenburg.'

'By nannies? No.'

'Kylie isn't a good example.'

'She's not, is she?' Tammy agreed politely. She picked up the book Kylie had been reading and grimaced. '*The Vampire's Slave*. A little bedtime reading for Henry—I don't think. You can see as well as I can that there's been minimal attention paid to Henry. He's had his physical needs met and that's all. And yet you employed her.'

'I was desperate. I had to find someone fast and I was on the other side of the world.'

'And it took you weeks to come and check on him. Great. Good worrying. Well, now he's in his aunt's care, so you don't need to worry any more.'

'You don't understand. I need him.'

She raised her eyebrows at that. 'You *need* a baby?'

'Yes.'

'Why?'

'He's the heir to the throne.'

She thought about that for a whole two seconds before rejecting it entirely as a reason for anyone needing a baby. 'Then he can be heir to the throne right here,' she told him. 'I'm not giving him back. He can ascend to the throne, or whatever he has to do, when he's old enough to choose for himself. But you—the lot of you—have shown yourselves to be incapable of caring for a baby.'

'And you're capable?' he demanded, goaded.

'Strangely enough, yes,' she flung at him. 'I'm even experienced.'

'I don't believe you.'

'Well, there you go, then. Distrust on either side. We make a perfect pair.'

This was getting out of hand. 'Can we at least talk?' he said urgently. 'Stay here tonight. I'll pay for a night for you in this hotel.'

Tammy took a deep breath. Anger was threatening to

overwhelm her. 'Gee,' she said, as if awed. 'In this hotel!
A proper bed, with sheets and everything?'

'There's no need to be sarcastic.'

'There's no need to be patronising.'

'You need to stay somewhere.'

She did. His words made her hesitate. Her fury and her
grief made her desperate to be alone, but Henry was cradled
against her. His belongings were piled on the armchair, but
she needed more than his possessions. She needed to find
out everything about the child she intended to take care of.
Things like immunizations, allergies... Maybe this man
didn't know, but somewhere there must be records. Maybe
she couldn't flounce out of his life quite yet.

He could see her weakening and pressed his point. 'Stay
tonight. Kylie can keep the child and we'll talk.'

'If you call Henry *the child* one more time,' she said
carefully, 'then I'll walk away and never look back. Henry
is Henry.' She hugged him closer. 'He's his own little person and it's time everyone started treating him as such. So,
no, Kylie isn't going to look after Henry. *I'll* look after
Henry.'

'But we need to talk.'

'Then we talk with Henry.'

'I can't.'

'Can't incorporate a baby into your busy schedule? Too
bad.' She looked around as Kylie appeared with the suitcase.
'Thanks.' She sat on the floor, perched Henry on her lap
and started tossing belongings into the case. She handled
Henry as if she coped with a baby all the time.

What on earth was her story? Marc wondered. What was
her background? Did she have kids of her own? The investigator had said she was single, but...

He knew nothing about her. She was still in her filthy
overalls, but already Henry was relaxing against her, leaning

against her breast as if he'd found himself somewhere that might be home.

And, looking down, Marc felt a tug of something he didn't recognise. This woman was as far from his world as any woman had ever been, he thought. All the values he'd been brought up to hold dear—all the values the women in his world set store by—they simply didn't matter to Tammy.

He had to persuade her to release the baby. He must!

She wasn't going to do it.

The impossibility of the situation crowded in on him, and for a moment he closed his eyes in sheer desperation. When he opened them he found Tammy looking up at him with curiosity.

'You're in real trouble, then?' she asked, and for the first time there was a trace of sympathy in her voice.

He might as well be honest. He had nothing else to lose. 'I'm in trouble.'

She regarded him for a long minute, and then seemed to come to a decision. 'Give me couple of hours alone with Henry now,' she told him, 'and then I'll stay in this hotel tonight. I'll take a room here, and after I get Henry to sleep we can have dinner together. Is that okay?'

It wasn't okay—it wasn't nearly enough—but it was all he was going to get.

'Fine.'

'Great.' She threw the last of the things in the suitcase and jammed it shut, then took the letter Kylie was holding and looked at it with something approaching fear. She stared at it—and then shoved it into her backpack as if it might contain poison.

'Okay. Let's get me shifted into another room, and we'll go from there.'

'You can stay here,' Marc said stiffly. 'There's no need to hire another suite. I'm paying for this place to the end of the month.'

'I'm not staying in your suite,' Tammy said firmly. 'I
have enough to pay for myself. There's no way I'm being
dependent on you, Your Highness. I'll take my own room
and I'll see you at seven tonight. Not before.'

And that was that.

As seven approached Tammy was more confused than ever.

Confused? That was an understatement. Her head was
spinning. Grief and anger and shock were tangling in her
mind like some horrible grey web, not letting her go.

But underneath… Underneath there was Henry. Nothing
else mattered, she thought. She'd booked herself a bedroom—not the suite Marc had tried to book for her but one
she'd chosen herself. Even in her much more modest room
the bed was king-sized. Tammy perched herself and the
baby in the middle of the bedclothes and simply sat with
him. She hugged him and crooned to him, and tried and
tried to make him smile.

He watched her with enormous eyes, as if she was a part
of his window—something to be regarded with vague interest but not interacted with.

She ordered baby food from Room Service and a grave
waiter appeared with a tiny bowl of stewed apple. She sat
Henry on her lap and his mouth opened like a little bird.
He was obviously accustomed to being fed, but not like this.
She played aeroplanes with him, as she'd once played aero-
planes with his mother.

He looked at the spoon she was waving in front of him
as if it had betrayed him. He was obviously accustomed to
being fed efficiently and fast—nothing more.

Undeterred, Tammy kept right on playing. She turned him
around so he was facing her and the spoon was spinning.

'Nope, Henry, you have to catch the aeroplane. Here it
is. Whooooo…'

The spoon spun in circles in front of his eyes, touched his tongue, darted away again, and then swooped in.

Tammy giggled and Henry's eyes moved to her as if she was the most mysterious creature he'd ever seen.

'Let's do it again, shall we?' she asked, still laughing, and the aeroplane started its tortuous circle again.

And on the fifth swoop...

Henry's eyes lit with what Tammy hadn't yet seen. A tiny gurgle came from deep within his throat and his rose-bud mouth curved up into a smile.

And Tammy reached out to hug him in delight and darn near burst into tears again.

This would work. Her world had been turned upside down, and she wasn't sure where she was, but one thing she was sure of—wherever she went, there went Henry.

She cradled him until he slept and then finally, reluctantly, set him down in the hotel cot. He needed toys, she thought. He needed—something. There hadn't been a single toy in that cold, huge room.

She could hardly bear to take her eyes from him.

But it was six-thirty. Reluctantly she showered and changed into clean jeans and a T-shirt, which was all her backpack provided, then hauled a comb through her washed curls and settled down to wait for Marc.

And to read her letter.

It was from Lara. Written four months ago, it had been stuffed in the suitcase and left unread for all this time.

It was important.

She was re-reading the letter for the third time when a knock at the door announced Marc's arrival.

For a moment she considered not answering, but then...he had brought her here, she thought. He had paid for a nanny for Henry. If it hadn't been for Marc, then

Tammy might never have learned of Henry's existence. The letter might have stayed unread for ever.

Henry's fate didn't bear thinking of.

She set down the letter and crossed to open the door, fury still her overriding emotion.

But the man on the other side of the door took her breath away. For a moment she forgot all about her anger. Whew!

His Royal Highness, Prince Regent of Broitenburg, dressed in royal regalia, was really something. But just plain Marc, casually dressed in jeans and an open-necked shirt, was something else entirely.

His hair was now ruffled and curled. His grey eyes were smiling, the laughter lines on his tanned face creasing into deep and delicious crinkles. His smile was questioning, and his eyes searched the room until he found the sleeping Henry.

Whew, indeed! He made her want to take a step back...

Or maybe he made her want to take a step forward—but she wasn't going into that.

'Henry's asleep already?' He was still smiling, and it was a smile that made a girl's heart do crazy things in her breast. It was *some* smile.

'Yes.' Her voice was more brusque than she'd intended, and she fought for something polite to say. 'Come in.'

'Thank you. I brought something for Henry.' He lifted his hands and there was a soft golden teddy bear. He smiled at the expression on Tammy's face and her confusion tripled.

'How...how did you know that's what he needs?'

'I'm not totally insensitive,' he said gravely. 'No matter what you think of me.'

Whatever she'd thought of him had suddenly changed. This was a sure-fire way to defuse anger.

'It's perfect.' She took the stuffed toy from Marc's hands and eyed the bear with wonder. There were teddies and teddies, but this one... He was small, and built so he was deliberately sort of scraggy. His stuffing was soft. His arms and legs were a bit loose and skinny—just perfect for a little one to hold on to. He had a lopsided grin and already he had a much loved look about him. For the first time since she'd met Marc, Tammy felt herself smiling.

'Where did you find him?' she asked.

'On my twenty-second toy store,' he told her. 'Or maybe not that many but it sure felt like it. Did you know there are a whole heap of very unsatisfactory teddies in the world?'

'There are indeed,' she said unsteadily, trying to swallow her emotion. She carried the teddy across the room and placed it next to the sleeping Henry. 'He's just perfect. Oh, Marc...'

But Marc was distracted. The room he'd entered wasn't to his liking.

'Suites have separate bedrooms,' he said, looking round in disapproval. This room had a bed and a cot, and a tiny table and chairs tucked into an alcove by the window. As a dining room it was hardly satisfactory. 'The phone call I made...I thought I made it clear to the management that you needed a suite.'

'I changed the booking,' she said brusquely. 'I want this one.'

'But I'm paying.'

'No.' She bit her lip, her pleasure from the teddy fading as the conflict re-emerged. 'I told you. I'm paying. I'm not being any more beholden to you than I need to be.'

He stared at her as if he'd never met her like in his life. She met his look head on, unflinching, and tilted her chin in an almost unconscious gesture of defiance.

And a glint of laughter flashed behind those deep grey eyes. Prince Marc of Broitenburg was amused. The peasants were clearly revolting, and royalty was pleased to indulge such idiosyncratic ways.

'Um…maybe we could get a hotel babysitter and go down to the dining room?'

His laughter only had the effect of increasing her tension—making anger surge. 'I'm not leaving Henry,' she told him, and watched his smile die. It was all very well for the peasants to revolt, it seemed, as long as it didn't interfere with this man's plans.

'The dining room would be more sensible,' he told her.

'No.'

'Miss Dexter…'

'You're not taking him,' she whispered, and they were no longer talking about where they intended eating dinner. 'I don't care who you are, and I don't care how many teddies you buy him. He's staying with me.'

'It's imperative for the country that he returns.' Marc's laughter had disappeared entirely.

Tammy hadn't been laughing in the first place, and she wasn't laughing now. 'It's imperative for him that he stays with me,' she told him. 'He's ten months old and he hardly knows what human contact is.'

'I can provide the very best in childcare.'

'You don't get it, do you?' she snapped. 'You can't buy someone to love a child. I don't have your resources, but…'

But he wasn't listening. His needs were urgent, and he wasn't interested in the issues driving her. He couldn't allow himself to be. 'Look, if it's a matter of money…'

'It's not.'

'I'm extremely wealthy,' he told her, as if he hadn't heard her. 'If I'm prepared to guarantee his welfare, to have child psychologists give him continuous assessment, and to give you this…'

He held out a slip of paper. A cheque. Tammy looked down at it—and stared.

How many zeroes? This was more wealth than she believed possible.

What on earth was happening here? This man might be so good-looking he made her gasp, and he might have a smile to melt ice, but all she felt was fury.

She thought back to the letter she'd just read, and a cold, hard knot of anger settled and stayed deep within. Money. This had all been about money from the first. Henry himself was the result of a desire for money and prestige and power, and here was this man offering more.

'You could retire on what I'm offering,' he was saying. 'You could stay in places like this all the time. You'd never have to work again,'

She took a deep breath, and breathed again. Then her eyes flickered from the cheque to his face—and he was smiling. The man actually had the gall to be *smiling*!

He expected her to accept.

And at that the knot of pain and fury stretched and snapped. She lifted the cheque he was holding out, read it carefully as if she needed to memorise the crass insensitivity of his action, and then ripped it into a thousand pieces. She let them fall onto the luxurious carpet. She stomped on them with her bare toes and then she stared up at him, her face a mixture of hostility and defiance.

He still didn't get it. He was staring back at her as if he didn't understand, and her fury was still there. The knot was coiling again and there was nothing else for it.

She lifted her hand and she slapped.

She'd never slapped a man in her life. She'd never slapped anyone. And now… In the course of three hours she'd thrown baby formula all over him and she'd hit him.

She didn't care.

'Get out,' she whispered, choking on her fury as she hauled open the door. 'Get out. If we never see you again it'll be too soon. You and your damned family and your stupid money…'

'What…?' He was holding his face as if he couldn't believe what she'd done. The peasants were indeed revolting. With violence!

'You killed my Lara.' She was stammering with rage. 'You took her life. You…' She raised her hand again but he was before her, seizing her hands and dragging them behind her back. A middle-aged couple were walking along the hall to their suite and they paused in concern.

'Is everything all right?' the man asked, and Marc swore through gritted teeth, pushed Tammy back into the room and slammed the door.

'Now see what you've done?'

'Spoilt your reputation? I can't believe you've never been hit by a woman.' She was verging on hysteria but she couldn't help herself.

'Believe it or not, I haven't. Until now. What the hell are you saying about my family?'

'I've read the letter from my sister. Sent to me four months ago.'

'So?'

'She was sending Henry to me.' He was still holding her hands behind her, she was pulled in hard against him, but whether or not it was to stop her striking him she didn't know. She was past thinking of his intent. Her attention was fully on the contents of that dreadful letter. 'Lara was frightened. She was in way over her head. Her husband was taking drugs. They were running with a crowd she couldn't control. He was always drunk…'

'I know that.'

His words shocked her. 'You know it?'

'Jean-Paul was a mindless, arrogant twit,' he said grimly. 'He'd been overindulged since birth. He was an alcoholic by the time he was eighteen. If you're thinking he changed after your sister married him then think again. She knew exactly what she was getting into.'

Tammy flinched. 'Then why…?'

'Why did she marry him?' Marc's lips compressed into a smile that held no humour at all. He stared down at the ripped pieces of cheque littering the floor and shook his head. 'Lara would never have done that.'

'Ripped your cheque?'

'Ripped anyone's cheque. She and your mother… I remember them at the wedding. They thought they'd won the ultimate trophy. And all they'd won was Jean-Paul.'

'She'd won the chance to be a princess.'

'It came at a cost.'

She was staring up at him, her breathing coming way too fast. He was still holding her, but absently. He didn't know his own strength, she thought. He held her as if he could take on three of her.

He probably could.

'Let me go,' she breathed, and he stared down her, and his dark eyes glittered with something she didn't understand.

'Will you hit me again?'

'Probably.'

'Then maybe I shouldn't let you go.'

'You could just leave,' she managed through gritted teeth. 'That'd solve all our problems.'

'It wouldn't solve anything.' He stared down at her for a long moment. They were so close. She could feel his breath on her hair. She bit her lip and stared straight ahead—at the fine linen of his shirt. His top two buttons were unfastened and his throat was tanned. There was a trace of wisping hair on his muscled chest…

The way her body was reacting was crazy, she thought frantically. She needed every ounce of concentration to focus on Henry, and yet this man had the ability to sidetrack her—to make her think about his body…

Henry. She had to focus on Henry.

'What did your sister say?' He put her away from him then, with a rough little gesture that made her stumble. His hands caught her again—as if he hadn't meant to be so rough. He righted her as he'd right a doll, then stood back and watched her.

'I don't have to tell you.'

'I can't answer your allegations until I know what they are,' he said bluntly. 'I think it's time for the truth. Don't you?'

'I…'

But she got no further. There was an urgent knock on the door, cutting through her attempt at speech.

'Damn,' Marc said.

Tammy didn't move.

'Are you expecting someone?' he demanded, but still she didn't move.

'Is everything all right in there?' It was a loud male voice, raised in authority. 'Miss, can you open the door? We've had a report of violence.'

Great. Security. Exactly what she needed. Tammy gave Marc a look that was almost triumphant and marched to the door. She swung it open to find two burly security guards on the other side.

'Miss Dexter?'

'Yes.'

They looked past her to Marc, standing behind her. 'Is this man bothering you?'

Yes. She should say yes. She should have them drag him out of here so she could slam the door behind him and that would be that. They could speak to each other through their lawyers.

'We need to talk,' he said urgently as she hesitated. She looked back at him, which was a mistake. His eyes were urgent and compelling, and sending her messages she didn't understand.

'Why?' she managed, and the urgency in his voice increased.

'Because you and I are all the family Henry has. Because, regardless of what you think of me, I care. Because I have responsibilities I need to face, and because Henry has a heritage neither of us can avoid.'

'Henry stays with me,' she said flatly as the security guards looked on.

'Can we organise a babysitter and talk over dinner?'

'No.'

'Do you want us to remove him?' one of the security guards said, and still she hesitated.

There was so much she didn't know. She glanced back and found Marc still watching her with the expression she was coming to know. Watchful and non-judgmental.

She'd thought when she first met him that he had a good face. Kind. Maybe she was wrong—her wrist was tingling now from the force with which he'd held her—but still he watched, and she needed to come to a decision.

She thought fast, forcing her confused mind to focus. This was a five-star Australian hotel. Henry was an Australian citizen. Marc could hardly drag the baby from her arms and remove him. If he was planning on removing Henry from the country illegally he'd hardly have gone to the effort of finding her in the first place.

No. This man was a Head of State. He'd have to do things above board.

He could try and persuade her all he wanted. She could afford to listen.

'We'll have dinner,' she told him.

'I'll organise…'

'No. I'll organise dinner. We'll have Room Service here in my room, where I can watch Henry.' She glanced back at the security officers and managed a smile. 'We'll be fine,' she told them. 'His Royal Highness has a temper, but he's trying his best to fit into civilised society. If he promises to behave then he can stay. You guys are on call if he steps out of line again, aren't you?'

There was a sharp intake of breath behind her but she didn't care. Serves him right, she thought, rubbing her wrist.

Serves him right.

'We're at the end of the phone, miss,' one of the guards told her. Clearly in this hotel they were accustomed to all sorts, and violent patrons were nothing new. 'Dial 8 or scream. Either way we'll be here in seconds.'

But they weren't speaking to Tammy. They were speaking directly to Marc, and their body language said they'd like to haul him out of there right now.

CHAPTER FOUR

'GREAT.'

'Great?'

'Do you know what you've just done for inter-country relations?' Marc demanded as the door closed. 'These people know who I am and now they're thinking I'm somewhere between Godzilla and Attila the Hun.'

'As if I care.'

'You might not, but I do.'

'Were there reporters out there with cameramen attached?' They were both past fury now, and moving on to a level they didn't know. Sparks were flashing off them like two electric cables coming into contact. You could practically smell the burning. 'Are the press in this country interested in the doings of some tinpot prince? I don't think so. Broitenburg is a tiny country. I think you have an exaggerated idea of your own importance.. *Your Highness.*'

She ended her words on a note of bitter sarcasm.

Tinpot prince... She'd called him a tinpot prince.

The words hung between them

With anger still driving her, she turned her back to check Henry. The child was obviously accustomed to sleeping through noise. Now he snoozed on, tiny lashes fluttering closed over his dark eyes. She'd wrapped him snugly in a blanket and he was using a corner of it for comfort, sucking it in his sleep.

Henry was the important one here, she thought, trying desperately to get her thoughts in some sort of order. Henry. Not some crazy foreign prince with an overblown idea of his own importance.

'Will you tell me what was in the letter?' Marc asked, and Tammy whirled to face him again. She had so many emotions spinning in her head it was hard to know where to begin. His voice had calmed, but *she* was still a long way from anywhere approaching calm.

He saw it. His hands came up in a gesture that said he wanted to placate, not inflame the situation further. 'You must be hungry,' he said softly. 'I know I am.' He picked up the Room Service menu and flicked it open. 'Let me order dinner for both of us and we'll eat and talk at the same time.'

'Here?'

'Of course here. You've made that plain.' He managed a smile. 'If I object your very efficient security officers will come and eject me. They'll create an international incident and that will be that. So… I'm in your hands, Miss Dexter.'

She backed off a pace and glared. 'Why don't I trust that smile?'

'You can trust me,' he said, so softly that she hardly heard.

But she did hear. She looked at him for a long moment. Their eyes locked and she found her colour mounting. This time it wasn't from anger.

You can trust me? Did she? What was it about this man?

'Fine,' she stammered. 'Order. Only not frogs' legs.'

'Or kangaroo steak,' he said gravely. 'Agreed?'

'Agreed.'

'At last. We have consensus.'

They might have had a consensus on dinner, but they sat at either side of Tammy's tiny table and eyed each other as if either could produce a loaded automatic at any minute.

Marc poured wine, and Tammy eyed that, too, with distrust.

'No, Miss Dexter,' he told her. 'The wine doesn't contain poison, and I'm not trying to get you drunk.'

'I wouldn't put it past you.'

Marc closed his eyes. When he opened them the humour had gone. There was bleak acceptance of where she was coming from.

'What was in the letter?'

'I'd imagine you know.'

'I know very little,' he told her. 'I had little to do with my cousin. Our families were not close.'

'How can you be Prince Regent if your families were not close?'

'I never expected to inherit the crown. Jean-Paul had an older brother, Franz, who was killed in a car racing accident five years ago. After Franz's death Jean-Paul inherited the crown. With two cousins before me I'd never imagined it could come to me. And I don't want it.'

She frowned. 'You don't want it?'

'Believe it or not, no.'

'So why…?'

'There's no one else,' he said heavily. 'Except Henry. Tell me what was in the letter.'

Tammy bit her lip. She took a sip of the wine, which was gorgeous—Marc certainly knew how to order wine—and thought about it. The letter was intensely personal, but maybe the time for keeping secrets was past.

She focused on the food for a bit: lobster and salad and fries. It was a combination that was just what she felt like. At some level she was very, very hungry.

But overriding hunger was the sensation that maybe she needed to be honest with this man.

There'd been enough secrets.

'My sister seemed…desperate,' she told him. 'Her letter sounds like she was way out of her depth. She apologised for not letting me know about her marriage and her pregnancy. She said our mother engineered her meeting with Jean-Paul and pushed them both into marriage. I can believe that.'

'I can believe it too,' Marc said softly. 'I hate to say it, but your sister seemed…well, she seemed a wimp. I only met her the once, at her wedding. She was a fairytale princess but a wimp just the same.'

'Lara always did what my mother wanted,' Tammy said sadly. 'From the time Isobelle took any notice of her Lara was her puppet. Fights are all that was ever between my mother and me, from as far back as I can remember, but by the time Lara was ten or eleven she was beautiful and she was biddable. Isobelle schooled her well in the art of making it in the world by using men.'

'So Jean-Paul would have seemed desirable?'

'Isobelle used to call Lara a princess,' Tammy said, and the old bitterness was still in her voice. 'She wanted it so much. My father was titled and moneyed, and for a while Isobelle thought she'd scored a title for herself. That was why she got pregnant with me. But even after she had me my father refused to marry her. It was a waste of a pregnancy so far as Isobelle was concerned. And maybe it explains why she hates me so much.'

'She hates you?'

But Tammy wasn't about to be sidetracked onto things that didn't matter. 'Isobelle married four times,' she told him. 'Lara was another pregnancy to force some man to marry her. And she succeeded. The marriage lasted for a whole eighteen months.'

'Lara was like her?'

'Obedience was her way of getting affection. We did what our mother wanted or there was no affection at all.'

Marc's eyes watched Tammy. He knew what she was saying. There was a lifetime of bitterness behind the words.

But he didn't comment. He waited for her to continue, and in a while she did.

'Anyway…anyway, as Lara got older my mother dragged Lara with her in her stupid schemes. Lara was too weak to see the pitfalls of the men my mother found for her. According to her letter, Jean-Paul scared her but she was too spineless to do anything about it. She let Isobelle push her into marriage. Then when Henry was six months old— they were in Paris and Isobelle had dropped in for a flying visit—Lara went shopping and returned to find one of Jean-Paul's crazy friends trying to feed Henry drugs. Jean-Paul thought it was funny. That was enough to get through Lara's thick skull. She wasn't bad. She was just…spineless.'

'So she sent Henry back to Australia with your mother?'

'She sent him to me.'

'To you?'

'According to her letter she asked Isobelle to bring the baby to me.' Tammy shrugged. 'I'm the one who's dragged Lara out of trouble in the past. Even though we were separated, Lara knew I wouldn't have refused.'

'But Isobelle didn't bring Henry to you?'

'No.' Tammy shook her head, still thinking it through. 'How could she have brought the baby to me? She would have had to find me, for a start. Then she would have had to explain what was going on and I might have yelled at her. It was far easier to dump Henry in a hotel with his nanny and tell Lara she couldn't find me. Or that I wasn't interested. Or she might even have told Lara that I was involved in caring for him. Heaven knows.' She bit her lip and her face hardened. 'Isobelle will tell me.'

Marc looked across the table at her, his face thoughtful. 'So there's no love lost between you and your mother?'

'None.'

'Lara's hardly blameless. Surely a mother would have checked on her baby?'

'By the sound of it…' Tammy said, her voice fading to a whisper. 'By the style of the writing it seems as if Lara was out of it, too.'

He thought about that and nodded. 'I wouldn't be surprised. If I'd had live with Jean-Paul maybe that would have been the only way I could face him.'

'He was that bad?'

'He was that bad.'

'My mother must have known.'

He didn't respond. There was no response to give. For a while there was total silence.

'Your fries are getting cold,' he said at last, and Tammy caught herself.

'I…yes.'

'They're good.'

'They are, aren't they?' she said, and managed a smile. He smiled back at her.

There it was again. That smile. It was a knockout. It brought sunshine where there'd been only blackness. It seemed as if where there was this smile her world couldn't be all that dreadful.

Not if this man was in it.

Now, that was a crazy thing to think, she thought savagely. This man and his family were the cause of all this…mess.

Henry.

Her eyes slid sideways to the cot and Marc followed her gaze.

'It's not a total disaster,' he said softly, and her eyes swung back to him in surprise. As well as everything else, did he have the capacity to read minds?

'Why do you want him to go home…?' She corrected herself. 'To go *back* to Broitenburg?'

'He must.'

'You surely don't want a child?'

'No, but…'

'Charles called you the Prince Regent. So that makes you the ruler of the country. Right?'

'Yes, but…'

'But what?'

He sighed, refilled his wine glass and settled back, like a man prepared to lay his cards on the table.

'The country is in a mess,' he told her honestly. 'Jean-Paul behaved like an absentee landlord for years, and so did his brother before him. The government's corrupt. Everyone who's anyone has made themselves positions of power. Charles, for example. Why does a country as small as Broitenburg need an Australian embassy? It doesn't. Yet here's Charles—being paid a sickening stipend, driving the car you saw us in, living in an embassy that would house a dozen families. Broitenburg is.. *was*—a prosperous little country, yet when Franz and then Jean-Paul came into power it was bled dry by corrupt officialdom. The whole thing needs a dose of salts.'

'And you're just the man to give it to them,' Tammy said thoughtfully, and Marc grinned.

'Actually, yes.'

'Why bother?' she asked curiously. 'Why do you care?'

'It's a wonderful country,' Marc said softly. 'I was brought up there and I love it. My cousins didn't give a toss about it, but Broitenburg under my grandfather's rule was magic. It breaks me up, seeing what's happening now.'

'So?'

'So what?'

'So why can't you thunder in and kick some butt?' Tammy demanded. 'Instead of throwing obscene amounts of money at me so you can spend the next twenty years babysitting, why not just go home and rule?'

'There's a problem.'

'Which is?'

'The succession is Henry's, not mine. The constitution makes me a caretaker monarch. When he reaches twenty-five, the job is his.'

Tammy thought that through. A twenty-five-year reign and then honourable retirement? It didn't sound bad to her. 'That gives you twenty-five years of playing king,' she said thoughtfully. 'Isn't that enough?'

'If that's what I have—but I don't. Not at the moment. My Regency only holds true if Henry's in the country. If Henry isn't living in Broitenburg then I have no power at all.'

Tammy thought about that for a bit more. She was still confused, and, as well, she found she wasn't sympathetic. She glanced over at the sleeping baby and the thought of Henry inheriting a crown seemed little short of ridiculous. Monarchies were all very well, she decided, but she was a modern girl. An Australian. Did a country really need a royal family?

'You mean, if Henry doesn't return the country would revert to a democracy.'

He shook his head, his eyes bleak. 'If it did there'd be no problem, but Jean-Paul has left the place to be run by power-hungry despots. I have no time to change things. Without a monarchy the country will self-destruct, and I can't let that happen.'

Help. The more she thought about it the more she didn't like it. Not one bit. 'So Henry needs to go back?'

'Henry needs to go back.'

She glanced again across at the cot, where the baby was still fast asleep. He was so little. He was so…needful. 'You'd put the country's welfare above Henry's?'

'I don't have a choice,' he said gently. 'I swear he'll be looked after.'

'He doesn't need looking after,' she blurted out. 'He needs love.'

'I'll…care for him.'

She stared up at him, trying to read his face. Once again she read sincerity. This was a man doing what he thought was best.

What was there in it for him?

The Regency. Twenty-five years of playing ruler of the country, she thought, and the idea hardened her heart. If Henry didn't return, this man would be nothing.

'I've told you—I don't want this,' he told her, and she stared.

'What…?'

'You're thinking I want Henry's return to ensure my own power base, but it's not true. I never wanted power. I don't want it now. If leaving Henry here meant Broitenburg could move into a progressive democracy then I'd leave him. You must believe that.'

'I—'

'But it won't happen,' he told her, overriding her interruption as he tried to give her a sense of his own urgency. 'The officials are ruining the country. We're a great little country, but whole industries are moving away because of government corruption. Good people—skilled people—are leaving Broitenburg because their skills go unrewarded.'

He leaned towards her then, his voice still urgent and his eyes not wavering from hers. 'As Prince Regent I can change things,' he told her. 'The crown has power—too much power—but in the short term that can be used for good. I can curtail government corruption. I can even rewrite the constitution so that the monarchy becomes more in line with the British tradition—where the monarch exists to lead the people as an inspirational role, not controlling day to day living. Tammy, you must give me this chance. I want my country to be the wonderful place it once was.'

There was passion in his voice. Fire. Tammy looked

across the table at Marc and saw a man who believed absolutely in what he was doing.

This man wasn't corrupt, she thought. He was honest and he was strong and he cared. There was a part of her that recognised something in him that was almost a part of her. Like twin souls…

For the first time she wondered about him. Really wondered. What had he been doing before Jean-Paul's death? Where had he been?

Was there a woman in his life?

Where had that thought come from? She gave herself a mental slap, hauling her thoughts sharply into line. This was hardly the time for wondering such things. He was pleading for her to hand over her nephew.

She couldn't do it.

'Maybe when he's older…'

'Tammy, he needs to come home now. His claim to the throne lapses forty days after his father's death. I have until Friday.'

Using her name unnerved her still more. Once more she attempted to focus on what he was saying. Friday. 'That's in four days?'

'Yes.'

'But…' She shook her head, bewildered. 'Why did you leave it this long to collect him?'

'I thought he was safe.' Marc's hands clenched on the table before him. 'At the funeral your mother told me he was being safely cared for in Sydney. She was so…'

'I know. I know what my mother can be.'

'I assumed she was going back to him. Heaven knows whether she said it, but that was the impression she gave. She acted distraught at the thought of her grandchild being orphaned. So I thought…I thought that he'd be best staying with his grandmother. I had to take urgent steps to ensure that I took control until Henry came of age so I put Henry's arrival down as something that could wait until the last minute. I had no worries about him—until I got the call from your country's Social Services.'

Passion gave way to anger, just like that. Isobelle had made herself an enemy of this man, and the tone of his voice made Tammy shudder.

'What the hell was she thinking of?' he demanded.

The answer to that was easy. 'Herself.'

Marc's eyes flew to hers again. 'You don't sound surprised.'

'Isobelle suits herself. She always has. Sitting around waiting for Henry to grow up so she can be a loving grandmother to a twenty-five-year-old prince is hardly her style. She'll be off with her next millionaire now.'

'You're not in contact with her?'

'I'll speak to her about this.' Tammy glanced down at the letter and Marc's anger was reflected in hers. 'Oh, yes. I'll speak to her.'

'But meanwhile…'

'Meanwhile you still need to take him?'

He nodded, anger fading to be replaced by determination. 'I'm sorry, but, yes.'

'And I'm sorry, but, no. I can't let you.'

'You must.'

'It's a dilemma, isn't it?' she told him. 'Broitenburg needs Henry, but Henry doesn't need Broitenburg. You might be prepared to sacrifice one little boy for the greater good, but I can't.' She bit her lip. 'Marc, I don't need to be a psychologist to see that he's damaged already. It's so hard to make him react. Lara knew what was happening. In her letter she's frightened; not for herself but for Henry. She asks me to help. She commits him to my care.'

'But…'

'But now I'm all he's got,' she said softly. 'I can't give him a crown or a country, and I can't save your political ideals. All I can do is care for one little boy, and that's what I'll do.' Her voice softened into compassion and she rose, pushing her chair back from the table. Decision made. 'I'm sorry, Marc. I'd like to help you but I can't. Unless I know he'll be loved, I just…can't.'

He rose, too. He stood staring down at her for a long, long moment, reading the resolution in her face. She wouldn't relent. Her face was grim and set. Implacable.

He'd never met a woman like this, he thought. She stood barefoot and bereft of any make-up. Her shirt and jeans were worn and faded. They were clean, but that was all that could be said for them. Her still-damp curls were trailing across her shoulders and he had the most impossible urge to reach out and touch one. Just one.

Impossible.

The whole set-up was impossible.

'I think we've come to an impasse,' she was saying. 'I think…maybe you have to leave.'

'There's one way out of this mess.'

'Yes?' She raised her eyebrows in polite disbelief.

He thought about it for a long minute, and the more he thought about it the more it seemed the only solution possible.

'You could come to Broitenburg with Henry.'

CHAPTER FIVE

IT WAS just as well she'd finished her fries. Tammy might well have choked. She stared at the man across the table as if he was out of his mind.

'Why would I want to come to Broitenburg?' she said at last.

He smiled.

There it was again. Just as she had herself under control—almost—that smile flashed out and it was enough to side-track her completely. But she had to concentrate. What he was saying was stupid.

'Why shouldn't you come to Broitenburg?'

'Because I don't want to.'

'Have you ever been?'

'No. How can I have been? I'm not even sure where it is. And...'

'There you are, then. It's the most wonderful country. Mountains. Lakes. Castles. It's like the Dordogne region of France, only better. Fairytale country. Tourists love us. You'll love us.'

She was still staring at him. 'I wouldn't.'

'How do you know if you haven't tried?'

'I live in Australia,' she said carefully. 'My career is in Australia.'

'When I first met you,' he said thoughtfully, 'you thought I was offering you a job.'

'I would never have taken it.'

'You'd had other overseas job offers?'

'I'm a tree surgeon,' she told him, not without a hint of pride. 'I'm highly qualified.'

'Despite leaving school at fifteen?' He was watching her across the table, his eyes thoughtful. 'I had a phone call this evening from the man I employed to find you. He's come up with a lot more detail. I know more about you now.'

She flushed, unnerved. 'S…so?'

'So you're probably the most knowledgeable tree surgeon in this country. You've done university courses by correspondence so you have book-learning *and* practical experience. You've even worked in Europe.'

'I…'

'In the famous gardens of France and England. You worked with the best man available. Lance Hilliard's reputation is second to none. You talked him into taking you on for three years and at the end of it you could name your price as an international expert. Yet you came back here.' His calm eyes were probing, questioning. 'But why?'

This was *so* none of his business. 'I love it.'

'I can see that you do. But why bury yourself…?'

'I'm not a people person.'

'I can see that, too.' He nodded, taking her objection for granted. 'But I can offer you as much isolation as you want. And as much work. If you're prepared to use your skills at the castle…'

'The castle?'

'The Broitenburg palace sits in hundreds of acres of cultivated woodland,' he said softly. 'It's very beautiful. The head groundsman would be delighted to have you work with him.'

She shook her head in disbelief. The situation was absurd. It was as absurd as this man was unsettling. 'This is ridiculous.'

'Why is it ridiculous?'

'Because I'm staying here.' She flashed a look at the sleeping baby and then glared back at Marc. 'I'm staying with Henry.'

'You can hardly take Henry back with you into the wilderness,' he said in a voice that was oh so reasonable. Oh so persuasive... 'Set him up in a tent at the foot of the tree you're working on? I hardly think so.'

'I'll take a break.'

'For a few months,' he agreed. 'Sure. Until your money runs out. And then?'

'Then...' She bit her lip. 'I can get a city job in one of the botanic gardens. I can put Henry in a crèche...'

'I'll fight you on that one. The heir to the Broitenburg throne will not be placed in a crèche.'

Anger flashed out at that. How dared he? 'It's no different to being left with a nanny in Broitenburg.'

'No. But if he was left with you in Broitenburg? Wouldn't that be much better for all of us?'

'I don't know what you mean.'

'Think about it.' Before she knew what he intended he'd taken her hands tightly within his. His hold was urgent. His eyes met hers and held, and the warmth and strength and urgency of his hold were compelling all by themselves.

'Tammy, the royal palace of Broitenburg is a wonderful place to live,' he told her. 'All your living expenses would be covered. We could find a really good woman to help look after Henry—you could help me choose her—and you could spend as much time with Henry as you liked. You could choose to be a lady of leisure...'

'No!'

'Or not,' he said smoothly. 'And if you wanted to work I'd be willing to pay you double your current hourly rate. More.'

She was staring at him as if he'd lost his mind. 'You mean I'd live in the castle?'

'Yes.'

'That's crazy.' She'd seen plenty of castles in her time in Europe, and she'd been fascinated by them, but they were something out of the past—a lifestyle she had nothing to do with. She looked down at the hands Marc was gripping and winced. Her hands were scratched and worn, weathered by the elements and by sheer physical work.

Marc followed her glance and his hold on her fingers lessened. He released his grip but traced the veins on the back of her hand up to her wrist. The feel of his finger moving with such delicacy over her roughened skin was somehow compelling. As if she was moving into a dream. Cinderella beneath the fairy godmother's wand. She was being drawn into fantasyland whether she willed it or no.

'It would work,' he told her, his voice growing more urgent. 'You could even enjoy yourself.'

'For how long?' She was so stunned she could hardly speak.

'For as long you want. For ever, if you wish it. Until Henry turns twenty-five and I'm no longer in charge.'

'And if I change my mind? Once Henry's in Broitenburg I'd never get him out.' There was no disguising the bitterness in her voice. She didn't trust him—why should she?

There was a long silence while he thought about it. He was still tracing the lines on her hand. He'd turned her hand over and was fingering the lifeline—as though he could read the future written there. As if he could read the decision hanging over them both.

'I'll make you a deal,' he told her at last.

'What sort of deal?' Her tone was still laced with suspicion. She was trying to block out the sensation of his hand— the sensation of his touch. She was using suspicion to camouflage it but she wasn't sure if she was fooling anyone. The way he made her feel...

But he seemed impervious to the ripples of warmth. The ripples of... In truth she didn't know what they were. She hadn't experienced anything like this—ever.

'I'll buy you both return tickets to Australia,' he was saying. 'First class. If I don't make you happy then you can come home any time you want.'

If he didn't make her happy? What sort of promise was that?

'Over there you'll have different laws,' she managed. 'You'll have Henry where you want—'

'I can give you solid assurances.'

'How?' She was being rude, but there was no option. She was fighting for Henry's future and she was the only person to do it. Despite the way this man made her feel...

He watched her for a moment longer and then he sighed. 'You won't trust my word?'

'No.' That was blunt.

'I guess in your circumstances neither would I.' He grinned, and his grin was as unexpected as it was gorgeous. 'Okay, then, Miss Doubter.' He hauled out his wallet and produced a couple of cards.

'I have legal contacts,' he told her. 'So far they've been useless for anything but telling me I wasn't able to take Henry home without your permission. But this card is for Paule Tarome—he's Broitenburg's Chief Magistrate—and this card is for Angela Jefferson, an Australian expert in international law. I'll get Paule to fax me an agreement, saying you have all necessary legal permissions to return Henry to Australia at any time you wish. Angela will witness it. Broitenburg is subject to international custody laws. If you're assured that I'm legally bound to return Henry to Australia whenever you want, will that persuade you to give Broitenburg a trial? For all our sakes?'

For all their sakes.

The phrase hung and hung. Still he watched her, his eyes compelling.

Somehow she met that look. She gazed steadily back at Marc and tried to read his mind.

She still didn't trust him. She couldn't. She *mustn't*, she told herself fiercely. No matter what strange things the feeling of his hand on hers was doing to her insides, this was Henry's future.

'Broitenburg depends on your decision,' he said, lifting her hand again and holding it in his. His touch was feather-soft. Pressuring but not pressuring. 'If you refuse then thousands of my people will end up in poverty. We need you. *I* need you and Henry needs you.'

Good grief. Tammy stared at the man before her and he gazed back as if he had all the time in the world for her to come to her decision.

Henry. Broitenburg.

This man.

Her life was about to change in the most momentous of ways. She had a child.

And Henry had a heritage, like it or not.

If she agreed...

If it didn't work then she could return and bring Henry with her. Marc would allow her to trial it and see if it was workable.

Should she agree?

Her head was spinning. She felt so far out of her depth she was in danger of drowning, and the concern in this man's dark eyes was her only lifeline.

She took a deep breath and made her decision.

'Okay,' she said, 'I'll come.'

He let his breath out in one long sigh of relief and there it was. The decision was made. 'You won't regret it.'

'I'll be the judge of that.'

'You won't regret it,' he said again. 'I promise.' He released her hand and hesitated, already thinking of the consequences of her decision. 'I'll need to make a few phone calls.'

Strangely, he sounded as if what he really regretted was being called away right now, and Tammy knew how he felt.

There was a part of her that wanted to stay exactly where she was—with her hand in this man's.

Which was ridiculous. Already he was working through the host of things he had to do before they left, but as he walked to the door, and then turned and looked back, once more Tammy sensed real reluctance to go.

'Goodnight,' he said slowly, and she nodded—an absurdly formal nod.

'Goodnight.'

'It'll be okay.'

'Yes.'

There was a long silence. Why didn't he go? Tammy thought. Why was he just standing there? He was looking at her with such a strange expression in his dark eyes that she felt her colour begin to mount.

Which was ridiculous.

She stared down at her bare toes peeking out from the frayed cuffs of her jeans. The silence went on and on.

And on.

And then, before she could guess what he intended, he swore softly and crossed to her side. In one swift movement he gripped her shoulders with his strong hands, bent his head to hers and kissed her.

It was a kiss to seal a bargain rather than anything else. That was what she told herself. What she assumed.

Or maybe she was so surprised she assumed nothing.

His mouth on hers was firm, yet it demanded no response. He was asking nothing. But…if it was meant to be an affirmation of the future and nothing more then why did it have the capacity to send a zillion electric shocks straight through her?

Maybe it was because it lasted too long, she thought through a haze of incredulity at what was happening to her. It lasted much longer than the intention of such a kiss should allow.

It had been meant as a seal on a contract and nothing more, but his hands were suddenly gripping harder, he was deepening the kiss, letting his body possess her for just these few short moments...

She was rigid in his hold, though her body was screaming to respond.

But disaster lay down that road. Tammy's world had been turned upside down this day, and the last thing she needed was physical arousal.

The last thing she needed was to respond to this man.

Yet her body was screaming to do just that. Sense or nonsense, her lips were aching to open and deepen his kiss. Her arms wanted to hold him. To draw comfort from him. To seek security and warmth and a lessening of this awful confusion and loss in his nearness.

In his body.

He felt wonderful. She'd never felt anything like this. His size—his maleness—his tenderness and his strength...

She was so confused she was near collapse, and when he finally put her away from him, holding her still but staring down at her in concern, he saw the depths of confusion and misery in her eyes and he swore.

'I shouldn't have done that.'

'I...'

'You've learned of your sister's death today,' he said grimly, though his hands still held her. Maybe if they hadn't she would have toppled right over. 'You've learned of your nephew's existence and you've learned that you need to leave this country. I'll take care of you, Tammy. I promise.'

The tenderness in his voice was so unexpected it took her breath away. She stared up at him and to her horror felt a tear sliding down her cheek. He saw it and raised a finger to trace its path.

'Damn, you're exhausted. I shouldn't have hectored you like this tonight.'

'No, I...'

'It's because I don't have time to take this slowly,' he said ruefully. 'I'm so sorry.'

Take what slowly? The kiss?

Arrangements. He meant arrangements to leave the country. The kiss had nothing to do with it.

Did it?

The touch of his fingers on her face unnerved her even more. Tenderness was an unknown quality to Tammy Dexter, and for good reason. She didn't let people close to her. Ever. She blinked back her tears, pushed herself away from this strange, enigmatic man and gave her face an angry swipe.

'There's no need to be sorry. It's not your fault.'

'No, but...'

'I need to go to bed.' She was so confused she was past thinking. She might not want to go to bed, but she needed to be alone. Desperately. Otherwise she might sink into Marc's arms and stay, never to move again. The temptation was almost irresistible.

And the temptation was crazy. Her sister had fallen for one of these men—these princes—and where had that got her? Dead, that was where.

The thought of that was enough to steady her, to make her take another step backward and to fix her features into a semblance of resolution.

'Leave,' she said.

'You'll be okay?'

'Yes. Just leave. And Marc... Your Highness... whatever I call you...'

'Marc,' he said, and he smiled—which sent her resolution into a tailspin, heading for oblivion.

'Marc, then. Just... don't kiss me again.'

His smile deepened. 'Why not?'

'Because I don't want you to.'

'Are you sure?'

She glared at him. Arrogant creep. Where was the tenderness now? He was a prince, for heaven's sake. Royalty. And she was a tree surgeon with bare feet and faded jeans and the worries of the world pressing on her shoulders. So finally she tilted her chin and did what had to be done. 'Yes,' she snapped, then stalked to the door and threw it open. 'Yes, I am. Now, will you leave or am I going to have to call my friends the security guards?'

His smile was still in place. 'I'm leaving.'

'Good.'

'Goodnight.' He walked past her. She was still holding the door wide, and as he passed he paused and tilted her chin. Then very lightly, before she could begin to prevent it, he touched her face again, tracking the path of one of those errant tears.

'I'm sorry I had to be the one to break this to you,' he said softly. 'So sorry.' He smiled, a tender magnetic smile of such sympathy that she felt her heart falter within her breast. 'Sleep well, Tammy Dexter,' he whispered. 'Tomorrow our future begins.'

His finger reached her lips and pressed lightly down—a kiss, but not a kiss.

And then he left her.

What had he said? *Tomorrow our future begins.*

Her future.

Until today Tammy's future had been so carefully planned, but now… She was leaving Australia to travel to a future filled with castles and princes and…she didn't know what.

Like it or not, Prince Marc of Broitenburg had given her a future she had no control over. She closed the door behind him and stood leaning against it for a long time, as if by doing so she could lock out his presence. The memory of him. The taste of his kiss.

'Be careful,' she whispered into the night. 'Oh, Tammy, be careful.'

Maybe she shouldn't go.

Maybe she didn't have a choice. And maybe she was glad of it.

The memory of his kiss had changed more than her future. It had changed her confidence in her own control.

Help?

The next two days were crazy.

Luckily she had her passport, and a visa was no problem. 'I do have a man at the embassy,' Marc told her. 'Charles has to be useful for something, besides spending my country's money.'

Tammy's boss was notified, and the sound of Doug's dismay overwhelmed her. 'You've got a job with me whenever you want it,' he told her. 'I'll even hold the baby myself if it means I can get you back working for me again.'

It warmed her. Tammy had worked for Doug for three years, and his workforce wasn't a standard forestry team. Doug actively encouraged women to work with him, figuring rightly that in this very male world the only women who reached Tammy's stage had to be good. Mia and Lucy and Tammy were an odd sisterhood, but along with the men they were the only real family Tammy had ever known. Tammy had held herself aloof, but the thought that Doug and the team would actually miss her—*someone* would actually miss her—was inexplicably comforting.

No one else would miss her. They wouldn't even realise she'd gone.

There was one really unpleasant call to her mother.

'Well, of course I didn't bother telling you of darling Lara's death,' Isobelle told her, and Tammy could hear the sneer in her voice. 'Why would I? It's not as if you cared for your sister.'

How little you know, Tammy thought, but she managed to hold her tongue.

'I'm taking Henry back to Broitenburg,' she said, and there was silence at the other end of the line. She could hear Isobelle's mind shifting from defence to speculation.

'You mean…with that prince who's ruling the place now? What's his name?'

'Marc.'

'Well, well.' The sneer in Isobelle's voice grew even more marked, and Tammy wondered for what must have been the millionth time in her life just why was it that her mother hated her so much. 'You'll never get him.'

'I beg your pardon?'

'He might be a catch, but you don't seriously think you can succeed?'

'I don't know what you're talking about.' But she did. Of course she did. Her mother had a one-track mind. Men were a means to an end.

'You're not pretty enough.'

'I don't…'

'And he has women. I've heard all about your precious Prince Marc. He's a womaniser. He'll eat you up and spit you out.'

Tammy thought about the metaphor and found it wanting. 'He can't do both.'

But Isobelle wasn't listening to her pathetic attempts at humour. 'The man's rich as Croesus,' she snapped. 'You seriously think someone like that would look at the likes of you?'

Okay. She'd had enough, Tammy thought bleakly. She'd let her mother know where her grandson was and that was the only thing she needed to do. She thought of all the things she'd intended to say, and replaced the receiver on the handset without saying another word.

She had too much else to worry about.

There was the small issue of clothes. She had jeans, T-shirts, sweaters and a rain jacket. It was hardly a wardrobe fit for living in a palace.

It was Marc who raised the subject. She hadn't even thought of it.

'Do you have a permanent residence somewhere?' he asked. 'Here in Sydney? Can I send someone to pack for you? Maybe we could ship a container?'

She stared. 'What are you talking about? A container of what?'

'Your possessions. If you intend to stay long-term...'

'You could ship my possessions in the bow of a very small rowboat,' she told him. 'My "permanent residence" is a room in a boarding house, and there's hardly anything there. I'll take a cab over this afternoon and close the place down—grab the few things I need. But it is a few. I figure I might buy a couple of new pairs of jeans when we get there. That is...if they have jeans in Broitenburg?'

'Yes, but...'

He was frowning, but Tammy was bouncing her nephew and didn't notice. She'd had Henry chuckle twice this morning, and she was working on a third.

'But what?'

'We have formal dinners at the palace.'

'*You* have formal dinners at the palace,' she corrected him. 'Not me. I've never been to a formal dinner in my life. If I have a microwave in my room and there's a supermarket nearby then I'm happy.'

His frown deepened. 'I intend you to be part of the royal family. Not a servant.'

'I'm not intending to be a part of any royal family, thank you very much.'

'Henry will be brought up as heir.'

She jiggled her nephew up and down and gave him a

hug. 'You know, somehow I imagine Henry's not really interested in formal dinner parties quite yet.'

But Marc's displeasure remained. 'I want some things clear,' he told her. 'You're coming over as a family member. As such there will be formalities you'll have to face.'

She thought about it, and was prepared to concede a point. 'You mean I need to do something about my shoes?' She stared down at her bare toes and then glanced at the door, where she'd kicked off her boots. Okay, she would have to replace those awful boots. 'I'll buy some trainers.'

'That's *some* concession.'

She grinned. 'Why, thank you—Your Highness.'

His scowl deepened. 'It won't work.'

'You're telling me I should go out and buy a tiara or two and the odd pair of stilettos before I get to Broitenburg?'

'It might be best. Maybe not tiaras, but…something a little more formal than you have on now.'

She shook her head. 'Nope,' she told him flatly. 'There's no point. Broitenburg's had Lara. It's had its fairy princess. Now it's stuck with me.'

He couldn't budge her, and in the end Charles drove them to the airport with a huge leather suitcase containing Marc's belongings, another containing Henry's baby gear—and a small battered backpack containing all that Tammy possessed in the world.

CHAPTER SIX

IT GREW stranger.

For a start they sat in the pointy end of the aeroplane. First class. Tammy had never sat in anything other than economy in her life.

Marc had booked three seats. There was a baby crib in front of them so Henry could be put down when he needed to sleep. There was room on the floor for Henry to crawl, and the stewards were on hand to cater for every whim.

But from the time Tammy entered the aircraft she felt as if she'd wandered onto the wrong movie set.

'Can't I go and sit in economy?' she asked. 'I don't feel like I'm flying unless my knees are stuck into my chin.'

'Stick your knees under your chin if you must,' Marc growled. 'But you stay here. If you leave me with Henry then I'll go into a spasm.'

She cast him a sideways look. He was eyeing Henry as if he might bite. 'Babies aren't your thing, huh?'

'They certainly aren't.'

Not for the first time she wondered about him. What was it her mother had said about him? That he was a womaniser? Maybe, but the description didn't quite fit.

Here in the forced intimacy of the airliner facing a twenty-four-hour flight, there was all the time in the world to ask questions. After all, what could he do if he was offended? Kick her off the plane? No way, she decided. He wouldn't even tolerate her going to economy.

So she could chance a few impertinent questions.

'You're not married?'

'I've told you I'm not.'

'Do you have a partner?'

He raised his eyebrows at that. 'A partner...' His dark eyes suddenly crinkled in amusement. 'You're covering all eventualities here. Do I have a girlfriend, a boyfriend or a dog?'

'Okay.' She smiled back. 'Any of the above. Do you?'

He thought about it for a minute and then nodded, as though the question was a bit of an imposition but he'd answer it anyway. 'I have a girlfriend.'

'I see.' A girlfriend. So what was he doing kissing her? Maybe her mother was right. He was a womanizer.

She shouldn't mind. She didn't. Did she?

'What about you?' he asked, his tone suddenly curious. 'My detective says you have no one.'

'It's hardly fair,' she complained. 'I have to believe what you tell me. You get me privately investigated.'

'That's what money is for,' he said equitably. 'But as for me... Since I've succeeded to Jean-Paul's position you need hardly hire a private investigator. Any European women's magazine will tell you more than you ever wanted to know.' His brow creased. 'You were in Europe for three years. I can't believe you wouldn't have heard about Lara. She was a real hit with the press—her wedding photos made the front of every major newspaper.'

'I would have been back in Australia by the time she was married,' Tammy said, thinking her timeline through. 'Back up a gum tree.'

'Your favourite place?'

'Yes.'

'Because?'

'Because people hurt,' she said honestly. 'Getting attached hurts. I tried with Lara and look what happened.'

'Yet you'll try again with Henry?'

'I have no choice.'

'You do have a choice. I told you I was prepared to bring Henry back to Broitenburg by myself.'

'And your girlfriend? What would she think of that?'

'Ingrid is hardly a baby person, and our relationship is hardly long-term. But you know I'd take care of him.'

'Yeah?' Henry was on her knee, sucking an ear of his newly acquired teddy with all the intensity of an athlete competing in a marathon. Henry and Teddy had contracted a case of love at first sight, and Tammy suspected Ted's ear wasn't going to make Singapore, much less Europe. 'You'd take care of him?'

'Yes.'

Right. She cast him a suspicious glance. The man looked immeasurably sure of himself. Capable of anything. Capable of caring for babies?

'Then how about starting now?' she asked him, and before he could demur she lifted Henry across so that he was sitting on the knee of His Highness, Prince Regent of Broitenburg.

His Highness, Prince Regent of Broitenburg, looked stunned to the socks.

'I...I can't.'

''You just said you could.' She closed her eyes with a determination she was far from feeling. In fact she wanted to stay awake and watch. But... 'I'm going to sleep now, Your Highnesses,' she told them both. 'Entertain yourselves.'

To her surprise she did sleep, and when she woke hours later the cabin lights were dimmed and the man beside her was asleep as well.

As was Henry. The little boy had fallen asleep on Marc's knee. The stewards had placed blankets over all of them. From her cocoon of blankets Tammy stared across in the dim light at man and baby sleeping together. They looked warm and contented, and very, very much as if they belonged together.

They even looked alike! Henry's tiny lashes were fast shut in an exact replica of his princely cousin's. His head was tucked under Marc's chin and, outside the blankets, Marc's big hand had a tiny fist curled around one of his fingers.

The sight was suddenly almost too much for Tammy. She gazed at the pair of them and found a lump the size of a golf ball forming in the back of her throat. Damn, what was it about this man that made her feel like weeping? This man and this baby…

She knew nothing about him, she thought desperately. Nothing. Except that he was Prince Regent of a small and lovely principality and he had a girlfriend called Ingrid.

'Ingrid is hardly a baby person,' he'd said. Was Marc a baby person? He hadn't seemed so. Yet sitting here, looking at the way the little boy was snuggled into him, it seemed there was a way into this royal heart. He might seem ruthless and overbearing, but Henry was exposing a side she suspected had never been exposed before.

Ingrid is hardly a baby person.

What sort of person was Marc—and what sort of household was Tammy getting into?

It was a household so large that it took her breath away.

No, she thought, stunned. It wasn't a house in any sense of the word. The limousine swept them along the vast curved driveway and stopped beneath steps that could have graced the parliament of a great nation. Below the steps was a lake, stretching away into the distance, and above…

Above their heads the castle soared skyward. It was something straight out of a fairytale. Built of white stone, three storeys high without its score of turrets and towers spiralling above, it glistened with a beauty that made Tammy catch her breath.

It wasn't ostentatious—or maybe it was, but it was built with such grace and charm that 'ostentatious' was the wrong adjective. It could only be called beautiful. Nestled against a backdrop of magical mountains, surrounded by exquisite gardens and woodland, the scene made her want to jump from the car and explore right now.

She could scarcely take it all in. In the foreground was the fairytale castle, all spires and gargoyles and terraces. Away in the background there were traces of snow, spider-webbing down the grander of the mountain peaks. The sun glistened down on the castle's stonework, making the ancient palace and its surroundings come alive with vibrant colour.

White swans were sailing across the lake in all their majesty. The grounds swept on further than the eye could see. This place had been neglected, Marc had told her, but Tammy could see no hint of neglect here.

Magic!

Her new home.

'What do you think?' Marc was asking and she turned to find him watching her with evident enjoyment. She flushed.

'I think…it's a ridiculous flaunting of wealth.'

'Ouch.'

'Pretentious.'

'Really?'

'And…' She could no longer prevent herself from stating the truth. She gazed around from the castle, to the grounds, to the lake and back to the castle again.

'And it's also very, very beautiful,' she murmured, and found Marc's smile had faded.

'It is,' he said slowly, and for a moment as his gaze still rested on her face she wasn't sure exactly what he meant.

Neither was Marc.

But Tammy couldn't dwell on Marc's thoughts. She had enough of her own to absorb. She thought back to the shabby one-room apartment that had been her base for the past ten years and had to pinch herself to believe she wasn't dreaming. And when a uniformed butler made his stately way down the steps and held the car door wide for her she had to pinch herself all over again.

'This isn't real,' she muttered, and found that Marc was watching her still. His laughter had faded completely now and there was a strangely enigmatic expression in the back of his eyes.

'It's real.'

'Welcome home,' the butler was saying, with all the solemnity in the world, and she closed her eyes and wondered what on earth she had got herself into.

Welcome home indeed.

The staff were lined up to meet them. It was like something out of a television show, Tammy thought dumbly, walking along the line of uniformed staff to be introduced. There must be twenty people assembled in the great hall. Marc knew each of them by name. He greeted them with what seemed to Tammy to be real friendliness.

'I won't be able to remember anyone,' Tammy stammered unhappily, suddenly acutely conscious of her shabby clothes. Maybe Marc had been right. Maybe one dress wouldn't have hurt. Or two...

'We won't expect you to.' Marc was smiling at her, with the smile that had caused so much trouble. Was it that smile that had made her agree to this crazy journey? 'But maybe you'd better learn the most important. This is Dominic, our butler and head steward. And, Tammy, this is Mrs Burchett.'

An elderly lady was on the end of the receiving line. She bobbed a curtsey to Marc but her eyes were on the baby in Marc's arms. Since the flight Henry had moved back and forth between the two adults naturally, and now he was cradled in Marc's arms as if he belonged. 'Mrs Burchett is our housekeeper,' Marc was telling Tammy as Henry gurgled his own greeting, 'and she's English. Anything you want to know, ask Madge.'

'It'll be a pleasure.' Madge Burchett beamed, her smile enough to lessen Tammy's feeling of intimidation all on its own. 'Oh, hasn't the wee lad grown? We haven't seen him since just after his birth. And you're his aunt.' Her eyes raked Tammy from head to foot, and Tammy could sense the comparison to her sister. Nothing was said, though, except, 'You're very welcome...?'

'Thank you.'

'Can I take you and the little one up to your rooms?'

'That's a good idea,' Marc told her. He tried to hand Henry over to the housekeeper but the little boy clung. Marc disengaged his pudgy hands from around his neck and passed him to Tammy. 'Madge, if you can look after Miss Tamsin...?'

'I surely can. Will you come this way, please?'

Tammy cast an uncertain look at Marc, but he was already moving away from her. He'd have things to do, she told herself. A million things. He'd handed the baby over to the women. He'd played his part. From now on, his body language said, he intended to lead a very separate life.

As if on cue there was a cry of pleasure from outside and a tall, lithe woman about Tammy's age came striding into the hall. She'd obviously been out riding. Her outfit was pure dressage—gorgeous. Her chestnut hair was twisted up into an elegant chignon, her flawless skin was beautifully made-up, and the smile she was directing at Marc was truly something to behold. She held a riding crop, but she tossed it aside and ran straight into Marc's arms.

'Marc. Darling! How wonderful to finally have you home.'

Tammy bit her bottom lip and turned away, to find Mrs

Burchett surveying the pair with every appearance of dis-approval.

'Well, miss,' the elderly lady said, dragging her eyes from them as if she was seeing something she'd rather not. 'You can meet Miss Ingrid later. For now you'll be tired of trav-elling and tired of meeting people. Let's get you and the wee one settled.'

'Tell me what the set-up is here.'

It had taken Tammy all of two minutes to know that in Mrs Burchett she'd found a friend. Jeans and faded shirts might be inappropriate for this castle, but it was obvious that Mrs Burchett had been afraid of Tammy being another Lara—or another Ingrid. Her relief was palpable.

'What do you want to know?'

'Everything.' They were settling Henry into the vast nurs-ery suite. Henry had been the easiest child to travel with, Tammy thought and the reason was obvious. He expected nothing. He didn't cry because tears didn't produce results. He'd passed between Tammy and Marc with no fuss at all, and all he needed for occupation was the ear of his teddy.

He should make more fuss, she thought savagely. He should know people. He should demand attention. At ten months it was unnatural not to. The more time she spent with him the more Tammy wanted to shake her sister—her mother—Marc—anyone who'd had anything to do with him.

'The set-up here is simple,' Mrs Burchett told her. 'Apart from you and Prince Marc and Miss Ingrid, there's just staff. Until Prince Jean-Paul's death we hardly saw any of the royal family. Jean-Paul and your sister spent most of their time in resorts that are a good deal more exotic than this place. We were too far from the major cities for Prince Jean-Paul. The last time I saw Master Henry was when he was two weeks old. The family hasn't been back here since.'

'Never?'

'Never.' The housekeeper shook her head. She gave Tammy a searching look, and then decided to be even more forthcoming. 'We run a good household,' she told her, 'but the last few years have been hard. Many of us weren't being paid. It was only the fact that many had nowhere else to go that made us stay. Like me. I was an assistant cook—I came twenty years ago to have a change of scene when my husband died. Normally I'd never have been promoted to housekeeper somewhere as grand as this, but everyone more senior left. It's only since Prince Jean-Paul died that things have started to be put back in order.'

'By Marc?'

'By His Highness, yes.'

She couldn't call him His Highness, Tammy thought ruefully. Maybe if he hadn't kissed her…

Maybe. But for whatever reason she simply didn't think of him as His Highness. She thought of him as Marc.

'And Miss Ingrid?'

'She's been here for three days,' Mrs Burchett told her and the disapproval was straight back again. 'She arrived to wait for him—so she said. She's been acting like she owns the place since she arrived. Like Princess Lara's moth—' She gasped as she realised what she'd nearly said, and bit back the words, but Tammy knew what she'd intended to say.

'Like my mother?'

'I didn't mean…' Madge Burchett put a hand up to cover her eyes, and when they reappeared Tammy saw tears glistening on her lashes. 'I'm so sorry. I'm speaking out of turn. It's just…I seldom see anyone here who's English, and we've been hoping for so long that the little one would come back here. It means everything to us that His Highness has succeeded in bringing him home. And it's not just me who's affected. It's everyone in this country. My tongue's run away with me. I had no business criticising Miss Ingrid or your mother. My dear, I never meant...'

'You needn't worry. There's no love lost between my mother and me.'

'Beg pardon, miss.' The elderly lady gave an audible sniff. 'But are you thinking you'll stay?'

'I don't seem to have any choice.' Tammy sat down on the vast and opulent bed in the room next to Henry's and swung her legs. Her toes didn't touch the floor. This was *some* bed. It was *some* palace. More and more she was starting to wonder what she was doing here. She had no role. Aunt to Henry? Here on a permanent basis? She'd be a fish out of water.

But at least there was kindness among the staff. Mrs Burchett might think she'd been out of line, but her welcome couldn't have been warmer. Now she was beaming at her with a smile that would have warmed the coldest of hearts. 'It's so lovely to see the wee one with someone who cares. We were *that* pleased when His Highness rang and said you'd refused to let Henry come back without you. It's the first time we've had anyone even hinting that they care about the baby's welfare. Poor little mite. And now...' She gave herself a little shake, as if she'd said what she wanted to say and was now moving on. 'I'll let you unpack and sort yourself out. Is your luggage coming in another car?'

'This *is* my luggage.'

The woman looked down at the grubby backpack in dismay. 'But, my dear...'

'It's all I need.'

'But what will you wear to dinner?'

'This. I intend to eat here. I don't want to eat with His Highness. Or...or Ingrid.'

'You can't eat up here.' The housekeeper sounded appalled.

'Then I'll eat with you, in the servant quarters.'

'That would never do.' The thought was clearly horrific.

Damn. Tammy looked around her at the lushly furnished nursery suite. It might be gorgeous, but it needed a stove and a fridge and a few basic essentials. And she just knew there wouldn't be a supermarket for miles! 'Can't I just have a sandwich up here?'

'Maybe for tonight...' the housekeeper said doubtfully. 'I'm not sure... Does His Highness know what you intend?'

'His Highness knows I intend to be independent.'

'And he approves?'

'It hardly matters,' Tammy told her, somehow managing a reassuring smile. 'I make my own decisions.'

'I'll send you up your sandwich, dear,' Mrs Burchett told her. 'If that's what you want. But what the Prince will say I daren't think...'

True to her word, Mrs Burchett sent up sandwiches and a glass of milk for her dinner. By that time Tammy had been in the castle for a whole two hours.

She was hardly at home yet. She'd spent the two hours unpacking—well, that had taken her ten minutes. Then she'd explored her surroundings. She seemed to have a vast wing to herself, and it was so huge it took her an hour of prowling before she felt she knew the half of what was there. She wasn't brave enough to leave her wing in case she never found her way back.

She'd fed Henry, whose time clock was out of kilter. He'd eaten and fallen asleep almost straight away. She'd showered, put on clean jeans, and then tried to figure out how she could stop feeling strange.

It was impossible, she thought, and when the sandwiches and milk arrived on silver salvers, complete with uniformed steward carrying them, she felt really, really ridiculous.

Worse was to come. She'd had one bite of a sandwich and there was a knock on the door. There was no wait for a response. Marc marched right in. He was dressed for dinner. Royal dinner. Dark suit, crisp white shirt, royal blue tie.

He was certainly something! He looked a real prince, Tammy thought, and tried to stop her heart giving the absurd lurch she was almost growing accustomed to.

He stopped two feet inside the door and stared at her sandwich as if it was personally offensive.

'What do *you* think you're doing?'

'What do you think?' She was perched on the side of her ridiculous bed and she waved her sandwich at him. 'Eating dinner.'

'Dinner's in the dining room. Now.'

'Nope. Dinner's here.'

He marched across and picked up her sandwich, inspecting it as if it was poison. 'So Mrs Burchett was right. You're eating ham sandwiches for dinner!'

'They didn't have Vegemite.'

He didn't even smile. He took a step back and surveyed her as if she'd arrived from another planet.

'Henry's asleep,' he told her, slowly, as if she might have trouble understanding the language.

'Mmm.' She smiled.

'So why are you sitting up here? Alone?'

'I told you. We keep our lives separate. That's the way I want it, so I might as well start now.'

'That's ridiculous. Mrs Burchett has prepared a wonderful dinner. I won't allow you to offend the staff.'

'Mrs Burchett sent me the sandwiches. She understands.'

'She doesn't understand anything.' He stood back and raked his hair in a gesture that contained both weariness and frustration. 'Tammy, it's my job to get this place running as it should. In my uncle's time this was a family home. The staff here nearly all worked under him and that's what they want to see. Normality. Most of them have remained loyal under the most outrageous circumstances. They're delighted that Henry's here and that I've elected to stay tonight as well. The least you can do is come down and enjoy the banquet they've put on for us.'

'Banquet?'

'Banquet.'

Tammy's heart sank. She stared across to the far wall. An entire bank of mirrors sent twenty reflections of her bedraggled self straight back.

'I'm not a princess,' she told him. 'I don't belong here.'

'Neither do I.'

'Yeah, right.'

'You're Henry's guardian and his aunt,' he said with an attempt at patience. 'You have as much a place in this house—in this family—as I have. You can't seriously expect to sit up here and sulk in your bedroom for the next twenty-five years.'

'I'll find a house.' She'd already realized the impossibility of staying where she was. 'This estate is enormous. There must be somewhere Henry and I can stay independently. A gardener's cottage or something.'

'Oh, certainly,' he said with exaggerated scorn. 'Henry is the heir to the crown. Are you seriously saying he'll live in a gardener's cottage until he's twenty-five?'

'I'm a gardener,' she flashed at him. 'What's wrong with that?'

'Nothing. But Henry's the heir to the throne.'

'If I hear that phrase one more time—'

'You'll hear it lots of times,' he snapped. 'Because that's what this whole thing's about. You think I wanted any of this? I have a beautiful property of my own, not ten miles south of here. Renouys is my home. That's where I want to be. I didn't want to be Prince Regent. I didn't want to be responsible for Henry. But someone has to make the hard calls. Someone has to care.'

'I'm only in this country because *I* care.'

'Then go the whole way. I thought you had more to you than this. Skulking in your bedroom because you're scared of a formal dinner...'

'I am not!' She was standing now, her face white with fury. 'As if I don't know how to eat with the likes of you!'

'What other reason is there for you to refuse to come down to dinner?'

She glowered. 'I have jet-lag.'

'Yeah, right. And I'm the King of Siam. You slept like a top the last six hours in the plane.'

'I did not.'

'You slept,' he said harshly, but a glimmer of laughter was returning to the back of his eyes. 'I should know. You slept on my shoulder while Henry's dampness seeped into my shirt. I have a crick in my neck and a stained shirt to prove it. For six hours I couldn't move—and very uncomfortable it was, too.'

'I did not sleep on your shoulder!'

'Shall we ring the airline stewards and have them adjudicate?'

'This is ridiculous.'

'It is,' he said politely, and looked at his watch. 'Ingrid and I are having pre-dinner drinks. Dinner will be served in fifteen minutes. I ask that you join us.'

'I don't want—'

'Neither do I. But I must. And I think you should make up your mind that you must, too.'

'I've only got jeans...'

The hint of laughter deepened as he surveyed her shabby self. 'Whose fault is that?'

She glowered even more.

'You'll come?'

'I...'

'You have no choice.'

'Fine!' she threw at him. 'Fine. I'll come to dinner in my rags and I'll disgrace myself before your entire staff and you can snigger at me all you want. Fine. Just get out of my room now.'

'I—'

'Get out!'

Fifteen minutes.

Help.

She could go as she was. She should, she thought grimly. She should do just that.

But...she was Henry's guardian. She had a place in this household until Henry no longer needed it. She should give it a fair go.

The glimmer of laughter in Marc's eyes came back to haunt her. Damn the man. How dared he place her in such a situation?

He had tried to warn her...

She stared at her battered backpack as if it was a personal enemy. What on earth was she to do? She just knew that Ingrid would be gorgeous, and playing beggar maid to a handsome prince and princess was not her cup of tea at all.

But Lara had lived here for a while, she thought slowly. Lara, who chose and discarded clothes on a whim. If she'd lived here even for a short time... She bit her lip, indecision playing over her face. Could she? Should she?

Why not? She was in a fairytale castle. Why not indeed?

'Call me if there's anything you want,' Mrs Burchett had told her. 'The bell connects to the kitchens. Normally I'd have one of the girls answer it, but tonight I'll answer it myself.'

She stared at the bell and then made her decision.

She was a long, long way from the bush. She was a long, long way from home.

*   *   *

Ingrid was growing impatient. Marc's steward caught him on the stairs and detained him for another few minutes, and by the time he returned to the drawing room she could scarcely conceal her annoyance. 'Where have you been?'

Her tone was proprietorial enough to annoy him. 'Inviting Henry's aunt down to join us,' he told her.

'For dinner?'

'Yes.'

'Does she *want* to join us?' Ingrid asked incredulously. 'I would have thought…'

'You would have thought what?'

He hadn't been expecting Ingrid to be here waiting for him. In truth he'd been looking forward to a few days to work things out before he contacted her. But she was here now, and the fact that he didn't feel like speaking to anyone had to be overcome.

'Well, her sort…'

'Yes?' He stilled, watching Ingrid. 'What do you mean— her sort?'

'Well, she's clearly not used to moving in our circles.' Ingrid smiled her gorgeous smile and her gentle laughter tinkled out musically in the beautiful salon. 'What did you tell me? You've dragged her here from the Australian bush? Darling, you'll be lucky if she knows how to use a knife and fork.'

'She's Lara's sister,' Marc snapped, and Ingrid nodded thoughtfully.

'Yes. Isn't it amazing? That those two can be sisters…? Lara was a beauty.'

'Tammy—Tamsin isn't exactly ugly.'

'No, dear, but those clothes…and those freckles…'

'Do you want to go in to dinner?' he asked shortly, offering his arm.

'You don't want to wait for our little mate from the bush?'

'No need,' said a dangerously controlled voice from the door. 'Your little mate from the bush is right here.'

She took his breath away. Marc turned to face the door and it was all he could do not to gasp.

How had she done this in fifteen minutes?

She was transformed.

Gone were her faded jeans and her old shirt. Gone was Tammy Dexter, tree surgeon. In her place…Tamsin.

The dress was deceptively simple—a sliver of brilliantly cut black silk. It had a scooped neckline and tiny capped sleeves. It curved into a cinched waist and hugged her hips to a short, short hemline. Her long tanned legs went on for ever to a pair of strappy black sandals that made her legs look even longer than they were.

And the rest… Her burnished curls were brushed to a shimmering glory, swinging around her shoulders in a soft cloud. She'd found some make-up—just a little—just enough to add a tiny touch of colour to her lovely mouth and accentuate those huge brown eyes.

She was stunning!

'Where the hell did you get the clothes?' he demanded, and her eyes creased in amusement.

'Now, here I was, wondering whether *my* manners were up to scratch.'

'I beg your pardon,' he said stiffly, catching himself. She was right. As a greeting it was hardly appropriate. 'I…Tammy, this is Ingrid. My…'

'Partner,' Ingrid finished for him, her dark eyes giving him a strange sideways glance. 'I'm very pleased to meet you…Tammy.' She came forward and took Tammy's hand in her cool grasp, gave it a lightly welcoming squeeze. 'How are you, my dear? We were just saying you must be feeling very strange. I wouldn't have wondered if you'd wanted dinner in your room tonight.' Her eyes perused Tammy and her look of light amusement deepened. 'You've been raiding your sister's clothes, I see. Well done, you. I was going to wrap them up and send them to charity, but if you can use them…'

The implication was obvious, and Tammy flushed. But she held her cool. This woman reminded her of her mother, and Tammy had learned early that anger wasn't a useful tool. Other methods were more effective.

'I'm pleased that you did no such thing,' she said coolly. 'I've yet to see the terms of my sister's will, but I doubt her private property would be yours to dispose of. Legal writs are so tiresome, don't you think?' She took the flute of champagne Marc had poured for her and smiled. 'Thank you. That's just what I needed. And Dom Pérignon…my favourite.'

Fifteen minutes ago she'd been saying that what she needed was a Vegemite sandwich. Marc blinked—but then maybe he would have blinked anyway.

Wow!

Until now he'd suspected Tammy had chosen her isolated profession because of an inferiority complex. Lara and her mother, Isobelle, were magnificent. They were creatures whose every feature screamed perfection, from the tip of their beautifully pedicured toes to their gleaming tresses. If Tammy had grown up comparing herself to such perfection—well, maybe anyone would have headed to the bush.

But Tammy was just as beautiful as her sister or her mother, he thought. Maybe even more so. She wore very little make-up and no jewellery, but in her sister's simple black dress she made Ingrid appear overdressed and over-made-up.

And Ingrid knew. And Ingrid didn't like it one bit.

'Well, of course if they fit you…' She was smiling, moving to the head of the table and gesturing to Tammy to sit.

Hostess to guest. The gesture wasn't lost on Marc who grimaced. Hell, he had things to sort out here.

But Tammy still seemed unfazed. 'It'd be a waste not to use them,' Tammy agreed cheerfully. 'By the look of the wardrobes I shan't need to buy anything more until Henry inherits.'

'You intend to stay that long?'

'Henry needs a mother,' Tammy said softly, sitting down as though she'd sat at such tables all her life. The butler was behind her—he assisted her into the chair and placed a napkin on her knees and she gave him a friendly, happy smile. 'I guess I'm it.'

'But if Marc and I—'

'Will you have wine?' Marc interrupted with a harried look, and Tammy gave him her very nicest smile.

'Yes, please.'

Hell.

Marc couldn't sleep. Finally, at about two in the morning, he rose and took himself out for a walk in the gardens. It was a full moon. The moonlight was reflecting off the lake and the night was gorgeous. He walked the full perimeter of the lake. His strides lengthened as he walked and so did his sense of unease.

What was he doing?

Until Jean-Paul had died his life had been uncomplicated. Or…less complicated. He'd been able to keep himself right apart from this family, and that was the way he'd liked it.

He'd been brought up close to here, but miles apart in terms of lifestyle. His father had been the Crown Prince's brother. The brothers had got on—once—but the children hadn't. Jean-Paul's mother had been a snob of the first order, who'd preened herself on her success in marrying Marc's uncle, whereas Marc's mother had been a warm, fun-loving woman who'd had little to do with royalty.

For good reason. At the thought of his mother, Marc twisted his mouth into a grim line. What they'd done to her... This family...

It didn't matter. It couldn't matter. It was past. He'd learned that the only way to cope with these people—with anyone who had any connections to the crown—was to be businesslike and brusque.

Because he loved this little country he'd do what he had to do over the next few years. He'd wear the crown and hold the monarchy in good stead for his little cousin, but that was as far as it went. If Tammy—Tamsin, he told himself harshly; he'd keep this formal—if she could be persuaded to take a royal role then he could step back into the background. Which was what he wanted. He wanted to go back to his lovely little estate and get right away from these people.

From Tammy?

Yes. From Tammy, he told himself savagely. She stirred him as he hadn't believed a woman could.

And he didn't understand why. His sort of woman wasn't like that. Not like Tamsin. His sort of woman was one such as Ingrid.

Ingrid...

The thought of her behaviour at dinner made his teeth clench. She'd been a bitch. He needed to get rid of her. After dinner, as she'd clung and expected to be taken back to his bed, he'd rebuffed her with more bluntness than tact.

'I'm jet-lagged, Ingrid. I need my own bed tonight.'

'I can just stay a while, sweetheart.'

Sweetheart... The term sounded almost obscene coming from her. She was beautiful, and she'd been an elegant hostess for him in the past, but their relationship hadn't lasted any more than a few short months. None of his relationships did.

That was the way he liked it. The women in his circle

were all tarred with the same brush as his aunt and Isobelle and Lara. He knew damned well what drove them. To bring a woman in from outside—to expose her to the goldfish bowl of royalty—would be to expose her to the same sort of pain his mother had experienced. He couldn't do it.

And Tammy...

Why did his thoughts swing back to Tammy? Tammy, gazing at him from that huge tree she'd been working on. Tammy, asleep on his shoulder in the plane. Tammy, hugging her nephew, making him smile, swinging her bare feet while she sat on that huge, crazy bed.

Tammy in the tiny black dress, beating Ingrid at her own game.

Yeah, right. Get involved with Tammy and he'd be involved with this family for ever. He hated it. Hated it! And Tammy was just such a one as his mother. There was no way he'd subject her to—

Subject her? What was he thinking of? Marrying the girl?

Where had that thought come from? Ridiculous! He was so out of his comfort zone in all this that he didn't know where he was.

'Damn you, Jean-Paul,' he told his dead cousin. 'I'm not playing your games. I'm not playing *any* games. I do what I have to do and then I get out of here.'

Tammy...

Don't be a fool, he told himself as he rounded the last bend and trod up the steps back into the castle. I should never have kissed her. God knows why I did. One thing's for certain: it's never going to happen again. She doesn't want me just as much as I don't want her.

But...how much was that?

CHAPTER SEVEN

MARC woke to laughter. He groaned and opened one eye to discover it was eight a.m. That'd teach him to wander round the lake in the small hours. His head was still in a time zone a thousand miles away.

Maybe he'd imagined the laughter, he thought, still hazy from sleep. One thing this palace never encouraged was laughter.

But there it was again, drifting up from under his windows. Definitely laughter. Tammy's?

A knock and Dominic was entering. The butler set his tray on the bedside table and started to pull the curtains. He smiled in sympathy as Marc grimaced.

'I'm sorry, sir, but you did organise a meeting with M'sieur Lavac at nine.'

'At nine?' Marc groaned again. 'M'sieur Lavac?'

'The accountant, sir,' Dominic told him in the reproving manner of a senior person to a child who has to be occasionally indulged.

'Yes. Right.' The palace accountant. M'sieur Lavac. Of course. Dominic was pulling aside vast brocade drapes and the light hurt his eyes 'Who the hell is laughing? Surely it can't be T... Miss Dexter?'

'Did they wake you, sir? Shall I tell them to stop?'

Them? 'Tell who to stop?'

'Miss Tammy and Master Henry.' Dominic paused by the windows and gazed down at the south lawn, a smile playing over his normally taciturn face. 'I'll admit I'd be reluctant to stop them. It does my heart good to see them here. We never thought we'd see a child back at the palace. And this aunt of the little Prince...'

'She meets with your approval?' The temptation was too great. Jet-lag or no jet-lag, Marc rose to see for himself.

They were right beneath his windows. A steep and grassy bank led down to the lake, and Tammy had climbed to the top, with Henry in her arms. While Marc watched she lay down on the grass, set the little boy down before her so they were almost nose to nose, held his hands tight—and they rolled down the grassy verge together.

Clearly they'd done it time and time again. They ended up on the bank of the lake, both bubbling with laughter, the baby holding his hands out for more. A cluster of ducklings and their mother watched from the water's edge, seemingly almost as bemused as Marc.

And for Marc it was a strange feeling. Incredible! He watched Tammy's laughing face and felt a surge of such desire it threatened to overwhelm him.

But this wasn't a desire he knew. It was crazily mixed up, he thought. His feelings for Tammy were merging with what she represented. Because in there, too, was a desire to do what she was doing—to play with the baby he'd already started to love.

Love? He didn't do love, he told himself, startled. He was there in the background to safeguard Henry's inheritance. That was all.

He didn't do love!

The butler was watching him with a strange expression on his face and Marc tried to catch himself. To appear nonchalant. He let the drapes drop back into place.

'Have the staff taken to Miss Tamsin?' he asked, as casually as he could. Which wasn't as casual as he'd have liked.

Dominic didn't notice, or at least he didn't appear to notice. 'Oh, yes, sir.'

With those three short words there was no doubting that Tammy had Dominic's entire approval. And that of the staff. 'Miss Tamsin was up at six this morning and she ate breakfast in the kitchen. We were shocked, but she wouldn't have it any other way. She brought the little one down with her and...well, by the end of breakfast Mrs Burchett says we couldn't have found anyone more different than...'

He faltered at that, and came to an embarrassed halt, but Marc knew what he'd been about to say.

'Than her sister?'

'I...' Dominic coughed and then met his eyes with honesty. 'Well, yes. Princess Lara wasn't universally liked. You know that. Prince Jean-Paul and Princess Lara never took it upon themselves to pay any attention to the staff. When they took the baby away Mrs Burchett and nearly every other woman on the staff practically broke their hearts. They'd been wanting a child in the palace for so long.'

'Yes.' Half of Marc was listening, but he was distracted. His hand had involuntarily pulled the drape aside again. It was as if he couldn't drag his eyes away.

They looked wonderful. Their laughter was infectious and he found himself smiling just to see their pleasure. Tammy was lying on her back now, holding the little boy above her at arm's length, crowing up at him as if they were both children. She was barefoot again—it seemed to be her normal state—and dressed once more in her standard shabby jeans and T-shirt.

In one sense she looked a pauper, but in another she looked a million dollars!

'Begging your pardon, sir, but will you be taking them back to Renouys?'

'Sorry?'

'Back to your own property. Will you be taking Miss Tamsin and Master Henry back to Renouys to live?'

'Oh.' Marc was still distracted, but he made himself think that one through. 'Why would you think I'd do that?'

'The inheritance clause you've told me about says the child needs only to stay in the country. Not here in the palace.'

'Mmm.'

'So we thought…the staff have been saying that maybe you'd be taking them back to Renouys to live with you there.'

'No.'

'No?'

'No.'

Dominic was still probing. That was the trouble with aged retainers, Marc thought grimly. Not enough respect. Dominic had known him when he was in short pants, and the demarcation between master and servant was growing more blurred by the minute. 'But you're not planning on staying here yourself?' He was shamelessly inquisitive and Marc grimaced.

'You know I'm only here until I get the mess that my cousin left sorted out. Miss Tamsin will stay here. There's no need for me to stay as well.'

'The place needs a master.'

'I'll be on call if you need me. I can't stay here indefinitely. It's not my home.'

'You're Prince Regent for twenty-five years,' Dominic said softly. 'For some that's a lifetime. You could live here.'

'I don't wish to.'

'But…'

'Dominic, no.' He was still watching Tammy, but the laughter had gone. The feeling of entrapment he'd had ever since Jean-Paul's death was threatening to overwhelm him.

'I'm sure Miss Ingrid—'

'Miss Ingrid has nothing to do with my decision on where I'm to live.' He flashed Dominic a suspicious look. The elderly butler could take liberties where no one else could, but enough was enough. 'Stop fishing.'

'I'd never…fish,' the butler said, offended, and Marc gave a reluctant grin.

'I'm very sure you would. What time did you say M'sieur Lavac is coming?'

'Nine.'

'Then I'd better eat my breakfast. And shower and change. And…is Miss Ingrid breakfasting yet?'

'No, sir.'

'What a shame. Well, I might have time for a quick walk before meeting M'sieur Lavac.'

'Yes, sir.' And Dominic turned away before Marc could see the involuntary smile that flashed into his wise old eyes. 'I'm sure that would be a very good idea. The south lawn is lovely at this time of the morning.'

The south lawn *was* lovely, but Marc hardly noticed it. He'd showered and dressed in record time, donning what were for him very casual clothes. Jeans and an open-necked shirt and that was it. He'd been about to pull his shoes on but suddenly thought, dammit, why should I?

So he headed down the steps wearing bare feet.

He instantly regretted it. There was gravel between the steps and the lawn. His feet recoiled in instinctive reaction and Tammy, strolling up towards the entrance, saw him and laughed.

'You've forgotten your royal slippers, Your Highness.'

'I often go barefoot,' he told her, but her smile deepened.

'Yeah, like I often wear a tiara.'

'Or elegant little black dresses?' Her smile was magnetic, he thought. Gorgeous.

'Sometimes it's necessary to wear what the natives wear,' she told him with dignity, and it was his turn to grin.

'I agree. Hence the bare feet.'

She smiled still more and looked down at her own bare toes. 'I don't think you should copy me. I'm hardly a native here yet.'

'You think you'll be happy staying here permanently?'

'Hey, give me a break. How can I make decisions like that already? I've only been here for one night.'

'But you like what you see?'

'I'm a bit worried about the standard of our accommodation,' she told him, trying to keep laughter from her voice. 'It's not what I'm used to. But Henry and I have been discussing the matter. We suppose we can slum it.' Her eyes twinkled. 'After all, if you can then I guess we can, too. No Antipodean's about to be surpassed in toughness by a Broitenburgian!'

She smiled once more, a gorgeous, all-enveloping smile, with lovely laughter lighting her eyes. And it set Marc back.

Henry was snuggled into her shoulder. He wasn't asleep but he was clearly a happy, content and tired little boy. The way the child's body curved into her breast did something to Marc's insides that he hardly recognised. Marc stared at the picture woman and child made and thought—it looked good. They looked so at home in this setting. It was as if the baby was meant to be here. As if both were meant to be.

Woman and child seemed made for each other, and Tammy was standing on the castle steps as if she belonged.

This could work.

He'd been staring at her for too long, and she broke the silence before he'd finished with his train of thought. 'Um…Marc, about a house of my own…'

He frowned, thrown off track. This certainly wasn't where his thoughts had been leading. 'A house of your own?'

'Okay, not a gardener's cottage,' she conceded. 'I see that such a place would be inappropriate for Henry. But for you to have me living here with you is also inappropriate. Last night... You must see that it can't work.'

He thought about it and disagreed. 'I think it worked very well last night.'

'It didn't.' The humiliation she'd felt the previous night surfaced again, and with it anger. 'If you think I'm going to play hostess to your mistress, you have another think coming.'

'Hey, Ingrid's not my mistress.'

'No?'

He flushed. 'Hell, Tammy...'

'My mother says you're a womaniser,' she said flatly, her anger fading as she searched for a more temperate tone. What she was saying was unpleasant enough without hurling it at him in fury. But she'd been thinking things through and they both had to face the truth. 'Whether that's true or not hardly matters, but Mrs Burchett agrees that you go from one woman to another. She says Ingrid's only been on the scene for a couple of months. She also says that now Ingrid's getting possessive you'll ditch her and there'll be someone else.'

It was so close to the bone that he almost gasped. Damn it, how well did the servants know him? And how dared this unknown woman throw his personal affairs in his face?

'This is none of your business.' He was almost rigid with shock and fury, but she didn't appear to notice.

'It's not,' she agreed, with all the placidity in the world, 'unless you try to kiss me again—which, if you know what's good for you, you won't. But if you intend to keep entertaining your women here—'

'Will you leave my private life alone?'

She had no intention of doing so. She couldn't. 'It puts me in an impossible situation,' she explained. 'Like—what was my role here last night? Guest? Hostess? Or was Ingrid hostess? She did her best to put me down and made it clear that I was her absolute social inferior. Does that mean every time you change girlfriends I'm to be patronised by another woman?'

'She didn't patronise—'

'Yes, she did,' Tammy said softly. 'You forget, I was raised with Lara and Isobelle. I can spot patronising from a mile off. And that's the lesser issue. You having one woman after another will give Henry the wrong moral values.'

'I don't believe I'm hearing this.'

'Someone has to say it,' she said flatly. 'If you want me to stay here then you need to find us alternative accommodation.'

'The palace is yours,' he told her, goaded. 'There's no need at all for these histrionics. I'm leaving.'

Silence.

It was early morning still. A gardener was heading over the far lawn with a wheelbarrow, and a couple of sparrows were engaged in an argument over the remains of a squashed worm right by Tammy's feet. Otherwise the world seemed to hold its breath. Waiting…

'You're leaving?' she said finally—almost conversationally—and he nodded.

'Yes. As soon as you're settled.'

'Leaving me here alone?'

'Not alone. With the staff.'

'With the staff.' She was thinking fast and was clearly unhappy with what she was coming up with. 'You mean you're intending to skive off and leave me with the responsibility for all of…?' She gazed up at the castle and then turned to motion to the expansive grounds beyond. 'All of *this*?'

No one had ever talked to him like this. No woman. What had she said—*Skive?* 'I'm not leaving you with responsibility for anything,' he snapped.

'So you're going—where?'

'I told you. Renouys—my own establishment—is ten miles south of here.'

'That's right,' she said thoughtfully. 'I'd forgotten. You're really a not important prince. So you'll go back to being no one in particular and operate your secondary role as Prince Regent on the side?'

'Actually,' he told her through clenched teeth—his anger threatening to overwhelm him, 'I'm an aquatic engineer. I design and advise on community water supplies, and I need to get back to my work.'

'How fascinating,' she snapped. 'You miss your engineering, do you? Well, can I remind you that I'm not just Henry's aunt? I'm a tree surgeon. I need to get back to *my* work.'

'You can. Right here.'

'But you can't design whatever it is you design here as well?'

'There's no need...'

'There's every need. I don't know the first thing about running castles. Nor do I intend to try.'

'You don't need to. The palace will run itself.'

'Yeah, like it's been running itself for the last ten years. Mrs Burchett's been telling me what a disaster it's been.'

'She's been telling you too damn much.'

'She's been telling me how miserable they all were,' she snapped. 'How everything's been pushed to the side. How Jean-Paul and his elder brother before him refused to take on any responsibility for either the palace or the broader principality. And here you are, ruler for the next twenty-five years whether you like it or not, taking yourself off from responsibility as fast as your legs can carry you. Landing me—'

'I'm still coping with the political necessities of the crown. I'm not landing you with anything.'

'No. Not with Henry?'

'He's your nephew.'

'He's your heir.'

'He's not *my* heir. Do you understand nothing about regencies?'

'I understand enough,' she said through gritted teeth. Henry had closed his eyes now, slumping down on her shoulder with the expression of a baby at peace with his world. 'I understand that your responsibility is this kingdom—this principality—for twenty-five years. I understand that this place needs a leader. It's desperate for a leader. I hadn't been here for half an hour before I saw that, and according to the staff in the kitchen this palace is just a sample of how much the rest of the country's in need of leadership. And off you go, heading back to your castle to be an aquatic engineer.'

'I don't need this. I never wanted—'

'What? Responsibility? Commitment? Mrs Burchett told me how you've been running scared of it all your life. She told me about your mother—'

'What the hell do you know about my mother?' He was almost speechless.

'That your father had an affair with Jean-Paul's mother and broke your mother's heart. That she committed suicide when you were twelve years old and your father drank himself to death soon after. That you blamed Jean-Paul's family—the royal family—for destroying your childhood.'

'I don't believe I'm hearing this.' How dared Mrs Burchett talk about him like this? He should stalk into the castle and sack her on the spot.

But…she'd only reiterated what every woman's magazine in the principality had been saying for years. Like it or not, this was public knowledge.

Tammy was backing away, her anger fading as she realised that maybe she'd gone too far. 'I know,' she conceded, a hint of apology in her voice. 'You're right in that your past history is none of my business. But I didn't have to be here long to see the staff are desperate. They want you here so much. They were trying to make me see…'

'Make you see what?'

'That you have to stay. They didn't tell me you intended to go back to your home, but now that you've said it—I guess it explains their attitude. They'll have known you intended to leave me and Henry here alone. Marc, I'm sorry about your past. I shouldn't have brought it up, but…'

But he was past listening to apologies. He was almost past listening—period. 'This has nothing to do with gossip,' he exploded. 'It has nothing to do with the past. I'm not a prince. I'm an engineer.'

But she couldn't let him off the hook. She couldn't. It was too important for so many people.

In a way it'd be a relief if he left, she thought. The man unsettled her in a way she hadn't thought was possible. But the alternative—for her to care for Henry by herself in this amazing place…

It wouldn't work. Henry needed her, but he needed Marc even more. For the little boy to be brought up as the future ruler of Broitenburg…

He needed Marc.

'You're the country's leader,' she told him, and waited.

'By default. Henry's the leader.'

'Yeah, right.' She shifted the sleeping little boy on her shoulder and gave him a wry look. 'Is there anything you'd like him to sign right now? Any acts of parliament you'd like him to draft?'

'I told you,' he said with exaggerated patience, as if he was dealing with a fool, 'I'll be ten miles away. I'll be caring for the political necessities. I can be over here in half an hour.'

'Your place is here.'

'No. *Your* place is here.'

'So you brought me here. Very good. Well done. But you're not skiving off.'

'I told you, I have no intention of skiving...'

'Marc?'

They hadn't noticed her, but Ingrid was suddenly above them. She was standing on the top step, staring down in amazement at the warring couple below her. Perfectly groomed in country style—a pale cashmere cardigan over an elegantly cut little tweed skirt—she was beautifully made up, without a hair out of place. Her eyes went to Marc's feet in horror. 'What on earth are you doing outside?' she demanded. 'In *bare feet*?'

He couldn't work out why she was so offended—whether it was because he was outside without her and talking to another woman, or because he was outside in bare feet. Despite the outrage of the last few moments he was forced to smile.

It was a very strained smile.

'Sorting gravel with my toes,' he admitted. 'I wouldn't advise it. Tammy here must have feet of leather. Good morning, Ingrid.'

There was no return smile. 'Good morning.' Her tones were like ice. Her greeting was addressed to Marc and only to Marc. Obviously she was still smarting from Tammy's responses the night before. 'I expected you in the breakfast room.'

'I thought you were breakfasting in bed.'

'I never breakfast in bed. The servants know that.'

He frowned over that one. *I never breakfast in bed...* 'How long have you been here?'

'Three days.'

He'd assumed she'd come yesterday. 'Why on earth have you been here this long? You knew I wasn't due back until yesterday.'

'Someone has to keep an eye on the place,' she said icily.

'It's your responsibility now, Marc. You can't let the servants get away with murder.'

'That's just what I was saying,' Tammy told her, sticking in her two bits' worth. 'Did you know his Royal Highness is hot-footing it back to his own property as soon as he can?'

'Hot-footing?' Ingrid's perfect English failed her at that. She stared at Tammy as if she was something that had just crawled out of a piece of cabbage. 'Hot-footing?'

'Going back there to live,' Tammy told her. 'He's planning on leaving me here—just to *keep an eye on the place*.'

'What? By yourself?' Her tone was incredulous.

'That's right. Well, just me and Henry.' Tammy smiled at the downy head of her nephew. 'His Highness says it makes sense. See if you can dissuade him, will you?' She turned back to Marc. 'Meanwhile, if you don't want me to start ringing up realtors looking for houses to rent, maybe you'd better address the problem yourself. You must see this is impossible.' She gave Marc her very brightest smile, dismissing him to a nicety. 'I'm sorry, Your Big Highness, but I have to put His Little Highness to bed. If you'll excuse me…?'

And she swept past them both with every appearance of a *grande dame*—bare feet and all.

For all her confidence in the face of Marc and his lady, Tammy was badly shaken. This palace was beautiful. This country was magnificent! But she hadn't planned on being landed as mistress of the house.

Was she supposed to take on the role of woman in charge of the destiny of the heir to the country?

She supposed she was, she thought, as she watched Henry sleep, and, being fair, it wasn't Marc's fault that she'd been landed with such a role. It was her sister who'd landed her in it by naming her as Henry's guardian.

Fine. She could look after Henry, she decided, but looking after the entire household and training Henry to his future role was another matter entirely.

'Would you like to check the dinner menu?' Mrs Burchett asked her mid-morning, and Tammy grimaced her dismay.

'Why on earth would you ask me?'

'I don't like bothering His Highness.'

'What about Ingrid?' Tammy asked, and the housekeeper gave a determined little shake of her head.

'It's you who's the mistress here now. We've been discussing things in the servants' quarters and it seems that's the way that'll suit everyone best. Now, what do you think of quail as main course?'

'I think chicken'll be better,' Tammy faltered. 'Because that's what I feel like right now. A chicken without any tail feathers.'

Lunch turned out to be a meal of solitary splendour. Tammy decided to avoid a replay of last's night's argument, and after Dominic announced 'Lunch will be served in fifteen minutes,' she arrived in time. She even wore shoes.

She couldn't make up her mind to be relieved or dismayed when Marc and Ingrid were nowhere to be seen.

'His Highness and Miss Ingrid will be lunching elsewhere,' Dominic told her in a voice that forbade further questions.

Good, she told herself firmly. This was good. This way she could get to know Marc's butler—a man she'd sensed from the first could turn out to be a friend. He'd been silently watching her at breakfast, but she'd felt that she was being judged. If she got this man on side he could be a powerful ally.

And it worked. It took all of the first course for Tammy to elicit a thaw in the elderly butler, but by the time she'd demolished the home-grown strawberries for dessert she was almost sure she could count him amongst her friends.

So where were Marc and Ingrid?

'They'll have driven over to His Highness's property,' he told her. 'Renouys. Although the staff would much prefer him to remain here, his Royal Highness doesn't enjoy this place.'

'Do you think you'll persuade him to stay?' Tammy asked, and the butler grimaced.

'I hardly know,' he admitted. 'But any persuasion you can add would be very much appreciated.'

Yeah, right. How was she going to do that?

She thought about it and she didn't have a clue. What she *did* know was that if Marc was off doing what he wanted she should do the same.

So after lunch she left a sleepy Henry with a clucky Mrs Burchett and took herself off to meet the head gardener. If Marc was off planning his future as an aquatic engineer, she told herself firmly, then maybe she'd better meet a few trees.

The head gardener was older even than Dominic. Otto spoke scant English, but he and Tammy had a common love of gardens. Language aside, here was an instant friend. The old man had been discouraged from doing anything new with the garden for years, but half an hour after they'd met they were poring over plans—Otto's dreams laid out for the garden of the future.

The plans were wonderful. Language difficulties were forgotten, and so was time as they strolled around the property, checking sites for every one of Otto's wonderful fantasies.

'This is amazing,' Tammy breathed as she stood on the site of a proposed avenue of Manchurian pear. 'Marvellous.'

'If M'sieur Marc permits…'

'M'sieur Marc permits,' Tammy said roundly. 'Of course he'll permit.'

'What does M'sieur Marc permit?' a voice asked behind them, and Tammy gave a start. She whirled to find Marc approaching through the trees. He was dressed in a suit, as though for business, and that was how he seemed. Businesslike. No nonsense.

But Tammy refused to be intimidated. After all, she'd seen him in his full royal regalia back in Australia, so how could a mere business suit throw her off-stride? The fact that the man himself threw her off-stride had to be ignored. 'Have you seen these plans?' she demanded. 'They're wonderful.'

'What plans?'

But Otto was already rolling them up, as if ashamed. Undeterred, Tammy took them from him and unrolled them, refusing to listen to his protests. 'Otto has so many things he wants to do in this garden,' she told Marc. 'I can't understand why he hasn't been permitted to do this before. Look at this hill we're standing on. Most of the trees came down in some huge storm ten years ago—at least I think that's what Otto's telling me. But no one's given him permission to replant, and erosion's starting to be a problem. We need to get onto this straight away. It'd be a crime if we lost any more topsoil.'

'A crime?' There was a strange look on Marc's face, but Tammy ignored it and kept right on going.

'Yes. And it's not as if money's a problem. Otto's has been propagating plants for years and has enough seedlings to plant a small forest. All you have to do is say the word and we can start.'

'We?'

Tammy flushed, but she couldn't deny her excitement. This estate was huge. There was so much to do.

'I'll help. Of course I'll help.'

'And you'll love helping?'

'Yes,' she said tilting her chin in an unconsciously defiant reaction to the strangeness in Marc's voice. 'I can help all I want. Once my living quarters are sorted out.'

'You'll stay in the castle.'

She closed her eyes. Here it was again. 'I won't stay in the castle. *You'll* stay in the castle.'

'This,' he said softly—dangerously—as Otto looked on in confusion, 'has the makings of a children's argument. *I will. No, I will.*'

'So stop being childish,' she snapped.

'No one's accused *me* of being childish.'

'I can't imagine why not,' she declared, her chin still tilted in the way he was starting to recognise. 'That's just what you are. Offloading your responsibilities onto a mere girl…'

'Now, that,' he said carefully, 'is nonsense. Has anyone ever called you a mere girl?' He surveyed her thoughtfully. 'I'd imagine you wouldn't have been a mere girl even when you were three. What do you think, Otto?' He turned to the old man and motioned to Tammy. *'Fantastique?'*

'Oui,' the gardener said definitely, grinning. *'Et belle. Très belle.'*

'That too,' Marc said thoughtfully, surveying Tammy with care. He reached out and removed a grass seed from her hair. 'Very definitely.'

'If you two don't mind?' Tammy said, flushing, and Marc smiled.

'Mind? Why should we mind? Two men discussing a beautiful woman…'

'Yeah, with grass seeds in her hair, a stained T-shirt and the knees out of her jeans. You're out of your minds.'

'I don't think we are,' Marc told her, his smile intensifying. But he needed to move on. 'Plans aside…and don't think I don't approve—I do…but I'm here to inform you that Mrs Burchett's planning soufflé as entrée, so we mustn't be late for dinner.' His smile turned quizzical. 'She also tells me she *was* planning on serving quail, but the lady of the house changed the menu to chicken.'

'I didn't,' Tammy said, horrified, and then thought about it. 'I mean…I did, but I didn't mean…'

'It's fine,' Marc said grandly. 'Planning gardens. Organising menus. You'll be at home before you know it, and then I'll be free to lead my own life.'

Oh, great.

CHAPTER EIGHT

INGRID wasn't there.

Tammy walked into the dining room and stopped, stunned. There was only Marc, standing in his dinner suit before the enormous fireplace, a curious smile curving the corners of his mouth.

'What?' she said crossly before she caught herself and made a recovery. 'I mean, good evening, Your Highness.'

'Good evening, your ladyship.' He gave her a formal bow which from someone else might be seen as a mockery, but from him was as natural as taking a lady's hand and kissing it.

Which wasn't exactly natural, Tammy thought, seriously ruffled. How many men had she ever met who kissed the back of a lady's hand? Approximately none.

And how many men could smile at her and make her insides do these really strange things?

'Where's Ingrid?' Her tone was more curt than she'd intended, and his smile faded.

'Ingrid had urgent matters calling her home.'

'To your home?'

'To her home.'

She thought about that. Part of her—the silly part—was very, very pleased. The other part had to be sensible. She should accept this announcement for what it was worth. 'So it's as Mrs Burchett says? You've moved on?'

'I've done nothing of the kind.'

'Will she be coming back? Ingrid, I mean?'

'I don't see that Ingrid's whereabouts need concern you.'

'It's only this dress,' she said apologetically, looking

down at the little black number she was wearing. 'If it's just you here from now on then I can go back to jeans.'

His lips twitched and laughter flashed into his dark eyes. 'Thank you very much,' he said. *'Merci du compliment.'*

'Think nothing of it.'

'I thought women dressed for men?' he said curiously, and she raised her brows in a look of incredulity.

'Only if they're trying to attract them,' she told him seriously, taking the champagne he offered and trying to keep her composure as their fingers touched. How he had the capacity to shake her just by touching, she didn't know. 'Which I'm not.'

Was that true? Was she trying to attract him? No, she told herself flatly. Or…not very much, anyway. Not any amount she was prepared to admit.

Somehow she made herself continue the conversation—which was really, really hard. 'Women dressing when there are other women around is a very different ballgame,' she managed. 'My mother and sister could dissect a woman's wardrobe from a hundred paces.'

'And you hated it?'

'I did,' she agreed cordially. 'Can we go find this soufflé? And this chicken?'

'Why did you knock back quail?' he asked curiously, and she flinched. But she made a recovery. Somehow.

'I never liked quail.'

'And if I do?'

'If you put me in charge of menus then you eat what I like.'

'You're a hard woman.'

'I am.' She grinned, suddenly enormously cheered by Ingrid's unexplained absence. It didn't make any sense, but then she was just about past making any sense to herself at all over anything.

* * *

It was a fabulous dinner.

The kitchen staff could cook chicken any night they pleased while she was here, Tammy thought dreamily. The chicken casserole had been luscious, as had the salmon soufflé for entrée. So was the flaky quince tart for dessert, and the tiny meringues Dominic was serving with coffee were melt-in-the-mouth wonderful.

This was like no food she'd ever eaten. Wow! She ate another meringue and thought the belt on her little black dress would have to expand a notch or two if things stayed like this.

'What?' Marc asked, and she looked across the table to find him watching her. This was a crazy dining room for just the two of them. It was truly splendid. Twenty-foot ceilings, gilded walls, crimson brocade drapes, a vast open fireplace, candles, paintings of ancestors looking sternly down, silverware, crystal, a vast silver epergne on the heavily ornate sideboard...

A woman might well be intimidated by all this, Tammy thought, and then looked into Marc's eyes and thought, No, *this* was what was more likely to intimidate her. Not the room. The man. Specifically, the way he smiled at her.

It made her catch her breath and more.

'I was just wondering what happened to the poor quails we were supposed to have,' she lied, and he smiled again—which made her catch her breath all over again.

'Do we care?'

'I *like* quails.' She forced her face into a frown. 'I don't like them to eat, though. I like them flying about. I found one once, when I was a little girl. He'd been wounded and lost a wing and he became my pet. Querky Quail. I loved him.'

'So you're not intending to eat Querky's relatives?'

'There's nothing wrong with chicken instead of quail,'

she told him severely. 'If I'd had to decide before either had been killed then there'd have been no choice, but if the quail have already been killed then we shouldn't waste them.'

'So you'll serve them up at breakfast?'

'Um…maybe not.'

But he'd come to a decision. 'Then you'll have to eat them by yourself for dinner tomorrow,' he told her. 'Or let the servants eat them.' He pushed his empty coffee cup away and rose to assist her to do likewise. As she stood, he pulled her chair back for her. Which unnerved her all over again. Good grief! A man assuming that she—a tree surgeon—needed help climbing from a chair? What next?

But she couldn't exactly say she disliked the sensation. In truth, it was an amazing feeling. For a start it brought him so close to her that her dress brushed the fine cloth of his suit. His hand brushed her bare arm and she felt a rush of heat straight through her body—a rush of heat she'd never felt before.

What was it with her? she asked herself desperately. She was acting like a teenager.

'I'll have to eat them myself?' Damn, why was her voice not working properly? Why was she finding it so hard to think past how close he was? 'You won't be here?'

'I'm going home.'

Home. Back to his own independent life.

That changed things. A cold, hard knot of anger settled in the pit of her stomach and the heat faded to nothing. 'Why?'

'I told you. I can't stay here.'

'But you live here.'

'No. *You* live here now,' he told her. 'You made that decision when you decided to come back with Henry. Your home is here. My home is ten miles away.'

'Then you brought me here on false pretences,' she said

angrily. 'Nothing was said about this when I decided to come. You made it sound as if your home was here.'

'If you hadn't decided to accompany Henry, then my home would have had to be here.'

'Then what's changed?'

'You, of course.' He was looking down at her, and his face was still. Expressionless. He was showing no emotion at all—in fact he was so carefully showing no emotion that she wondered just what was going on behind that carefully maintained façade. 'You,' he repeated. 'And me.'

'I don't know what you mean.' He was far too close for comfort, and suddenly she was finding it hard to breathe.

'You've said it's impossible.' Still that expression that said he was holding himself under rigid control.

'So it is,' she managed. Damn, she was still too close. *He* was still too close! 'I need my own space.'

'So do I.'

'Surely this castle is big enough for both of us?' She felt suddenly desperate. Overwhelmed by the enormity of what he was suggesting. That she be left alone... 'If you'll agree to me turning part of it into a self-contained apartment...'

'I won't do that. It's not necessary. I hate this place.'

She eyed him with caution. There was still no emotion on his face at all. Hate? He said the word like a carefully rehearsed line in a play.

'So you farm out your responsibility...?'

'I do nothing of the kind. It's not my responsibility.'

'Neither is it mine.'

'You chose to come here,' he told her.

'I chose to care for Henry. Not your whole damned castle. Not your whole damned kingdom.'

'Principality,' he snapped, and she gasped.

'Oh, for heaven's sake. I'm trying to be serious and you're fiddling with semantics.'

'I'm not fiddling with anything. I'm leaving.'

'You never said you were leaving so soon.' They were standing chest to breast, anger emanating from each in waves. 'I can't take on the castle. It's way too soon. I'm hardly accustomed to Henry yet.'

'It doesn't matter. Dominic and Madge will help you through.'

'So why won't you stay longer?'

'I have to leave.'

'Why?' She was practically yelling as she battled something she hardly understood. 'Why do you have to leave? What do you mean—you and me? Why are you running? Is it this castle? For heaven's sake, you'd think there were ghosts here.'

His face set. Hardened. 'Now you're being ridiculous. I'm not afraid of ghosts.'

'Then what *are* you scared of?'

'Nothing,' he snapped. 'I have responsibilities at my own château.'

'Which can't be handled from here? I don't believe you.'

'Believe it or not, it's the way it is.'

'No,' she snapped. She was breathing hard, trying to work things out in her mind. It wasn't making the tiniest bit of sense. 'Before we left Australia there wasn't a hint that you weren't staying here. Now you say you're leaving tomorrow. There must be a reason why you're going so fast. For heaven's sake, why?'

Why?

The word hung around them. The whole world seemed to draw in its breath, waiting for his response.

Why?

He stared down at her, goaded beyond belief. Why?

She was gazing up at him, her brown eyes dark with anger. Her skin was flushed. Her breast was rising and falling in angry passion, and her brilliant curls were tumbling onto her bare shoulders. She looked...

She looked…

It was too much.

Why?

He knew exactly why, and he could bear it not one minute longer.

He'd sworn not to. The first time had been a damnable mistake. He never should have done it. She'd been too sweet, too vulnerable, too… Too Tammy.

But how could he not? She was here in his hands, gazing up at him, and this thing between them…

He didn't understand it one bit, but he knew what he had to do.

Of course.

Once again he kissed her.

Afterwards he couldn't believe he'd done it. It was the last thing he wanted—wasn't it?

Of course it was. He'd kissed her back in Australia and it had been a mistake. Then he'd kissed her as an affirmation of a promise. But this…this was no affirmation. This was the age-old attraction between man and woman. Quite simply he wanted her as he'd never wanted a woman in his life.

Sense had nothing to do with it. Logic had flown out through the vast French windows. He was crushing her to him with a longing and a passion that had nothing to do with any sense or logic or…or anything.

For now there was only his absolute need.

He needed her. For this moment he needed her like life itself. She was his home. His heart. His life.

His hands gripped her with the fierceness of possession, and in joy he felt her melting into him. Her face was tilting up to his and it seemed she was as desperate as he was— desperate to find his mouth—desperate to reach *him*.

She was responding! Her lips were beneath his. Her

mouth was opening, demanding, searching for something that he'd thought was only his to need—but it seemed the need was hers as well.

This woman was his life, he thought incredulously. He could feel it. She was the other half of his whole. When she smiled, her smile reached his heart in a way it had never been reached. Ever. She was wild and free and untrammelled. Bare of make-up, no pretence about her, fiercely independent...

Yet when she held her little nephew there was such softness about her that she melted his bitter heart.

All through this dinner he'd sat, and he'd wanted her. Worse. All through this day—or had it started on the aeroplane, or even before? The sight of her bare toes on the grass this morning. The thought of her smiling down at him from that damned tree when he'd first seen her.

He was wild with the wanting of her. She should push him away, he thought fiercely. She should fight him. But her body was yielding to his with such infinite sweetness that he practically groaned aloud.

She set him on fire. All he could feel was the wanting, and a fierce heat was coursing through every part of his body. His hands gripped her shoulders tighter and then slid downward. As if compelled, his fingers moved so that he could feel the soft swell of her breasts. The perfect symmetry of her... The perfection...

Tammy.

Had he said her name aloud? He scarcely knew. All he knew was that his body was dissolving in a surge of desire he scarcely recognised.

This wasn't like him. He didn't feel like this about women. He didn't!

Oh, Lord, her own hands were moving now. He felt a tug and her fingers were sliding under his shirt, feeling the strong contours of his back. Teasing him. Wanting him as he wanted her. Aching for him. He could feel her need.

She wanted him as much as he wanted her!

He was powerless to stop. He'd been holding himself in a grip of iron all day. He'd been telling himself that he had to get away. One more day, he'd told himself. One more night and then he'd leave and see her only on formal occasions.

But how could he leave? He couldn't even put her away from him. Not when she clung to him with such passion— such a fierce wanting—as though she recognised that here was her mate.

Here was his home.

It was a ridiculous thought, a ridiculous feeling surfacing over and over, but he was beyond reason. His mouth was plundering hers and the feel of her was setting him on fire. All he knew was the wanting, and the heat of his need was throbbing through every vein of his body. The iron control he'd held himself under for all these years had slipped away at her touch. One touch...

One woman...

His!

The knocking took a while to penetrate.

For a moment Marc thought it was nothing but his own heartbeat, but there was another sharp rapping at the door and then a wail. Somehow it registered. Somehow.

Someone was knocking on the other side of the great doors.

Marc pulled away, but afterwards he never knew how. It was a sheer physical wrench, like losing part of himself, and he stood back and looked at the girl before him, saw his own confusion mirrored in her eyes.

'I...' He was staring as if he'd never seen her before. 'Hell, Tammy...'

'I know.' Somehow she managed a whisper. She put her

hand up to her lips as if she couldn't believe what had just occurred. 'You…you didn't mean to do that.'

'No, I…'

The knocking sounded again. Marc pulled himself together—a little—and turned to face the door.

'Yes?' When no one answered, he forced himself to take a step away and haul it open.

Out in the hall Mrs Burchett was carrying a wide-awake Henry. As the doors swung wide she looked from Tammy to Marc, obviously aching to know what she'd interrupted.

Obviously guessing…

'I'm so sorry, but…'

Henry had been crying—or maybe that was an understatement. His little face was crumpled and sodden, and as soon as he saw Tammy he reached out as if he was desperate.

'He woke and he won't stop crying,' Mrs Burchett told them. 'Nothing I do is right. He slept all afternoon while you were out with your trees, and now…he's wide awake and frantic.'

'Give him to me.'

Despite her confusion, despite the fact that her world had been tilted so far on its axis that she was in danger of falling off, Tammy's heart turned over. This was the first sign that Henry even recognised her. At ten months old a baby should be bonding with his people. He'd never bonded with anyone. She cast Marc a confused and desperate glance, but she forced herself to focus on her little nephew. 'Come here, sweetheart,' she whispered, lifting him from Mrs Burchett's arms and hugging him close. 'I…I was just coming.'

'Stay,' Marc managed. 'We need to talk.'

'I need to see to Henry.'

'You can cuddle him here.'

'We'll talk in the morning.'

'I'll be gone in the morning,' he told her, and that stopped her in her tracks.

'Gone?'

'I told you. I'm leaving.'

'But…' Mrs Burchett was looking from one to another, her curiosity a tangible thing, but it couldn't matter. Tammy was so confused she didn't care who heard the distress and confusion in her voice.

'You haven't told us that, sir,' Mrs Burchett said, and Tammy was suddenly grateful. Grateful that she could bury her face in Henry's hair and hide her surging colour while Marc had to concentrate on someone other than her.

'I've only just decided,' Marc snapped. Like Tammy, he was thoroughly confused. Hell, he needed to get away from here. He was losing his mind. He'd overstepped some boundary he hadn't known was there, and beyond the boundary was a chasm he was fearful of facing.

The chasm was so deep he might fall for ever.

Maybe staying and talking to Tammy was a bad idea. Maybe staying within fifty yards of Tammy was a nightmare.

'I'll see you at breakfast,' he said a trifle unsteadily, and made to pass by Tammy and the child.

But Henry was resting on Tammy's hip, and as he passed he brushed the little boy. Henry leaned back and held out his arms.

To him.

Marc stopped dead.

None of them could believe it. Tammy was holding Henry close, but the tiny boy was leaning back now, his face brushing Marc's dinner jacket and his tear-drenched eyes gazing up at his big cousin.

He'd bonded to the two of them, Tammy thought incredulously. Somehow over the long journey, when Marc had held him close and let him sleep in his arms, the baby had decided that here was a person he could trust.

'I need to...' Marc was trying to leave, but his feet wouldn't move. His eyes were on Henry, and they mirrored Tammy's disbelief.

And Tammy came to a decision faster than she'd come to a decision in her life.

'No,' she said, and before Marc knew what she was about she'd handed over her nephew. Marc's arms came involuntarily out to grasp the baby—to stop him falling—but Tammy was sure he wouldn't fall. She knew that this big man would hold his baby cousin and care for him.

She knew.

'No,' she said again, and took a deep breath. 'If you're leaving in the morning then tonight's your turn. You look after Henry. He wants you and I want my bed. Mrs Burchett, could I see you outside for a moment, please?' She grasped the housekeeper's hand and tugged her to the door. 'Goodnight, Your Highnesses.'

And without another word she slipped out of the room and fled, towing the housekeeper behind her.

Nobody was around.

At first bemused, and then occupied by Henry's need for reassurance, Marc took a few minutes before he left the dining room. Finally, with Henry snuggled against his chest and clearly contented, he tugged the servants' bell.

No one appeared.

'Let's find Mrs Burchett,' he told Henry, but Madge was nowhere to be found. The kitchen was empty. Coffee cups lay unwashed, but everything else was cleared, ready for breakfast next morning.

There were always servants around, he thought, puzzled. Marc pressed the nearest bell and waited.

Nothing.

'They can't all be in bed.' In the times he'd stayed in this palace he wouldn't have noticed if there was one footman or a dozen, but that there were now none was clearly unusual. 'Maybe they all go to bed at ten. Maybe I just haven't noticed before.'

Henry was gurgling happily in his arms now, enjoying this tour of the servants' quarters with one of his two favourite people. More and more bemused, Marc carried Henry out into the hall. On the table was a note, formally addressed to His Highness, Marc, Prince Regent of Broitenburg.

It was Tammy's handwriting. Of course.

Dear Marc
I'm only just figuring it out, but I'm starting to think Henry needs you more than he needs me—so it's a shame for you to leave and have him forget you. The answer is to share the parenting. Tonight you look after Henry. Tomorrow night he can stay with me. The night after that he's yours again. I know it's not perfect, but it's surely better than him losing you altogether.
Good luck. Tammy.

And underneath was a postscript.

As you tell me that I'm in charge, I've ordered the staff to bed.

Marc stood and stared at the note for far longer than he needed. Finally Henry grabbed it and started determinedly chewing.

Caring for Henry every second day? What was she thinking of?

Back in Australia he'd promised to care for him, he thought, dazed by where these arrangements were heading.

He'd told her that if she allowed him to bring Henry to Broitenburg then he'd be responsible for him. But he'd intended handing the little boy to Mrs Burchett and a hired nanny while he kept his distance. Madge would ensure Henry had everything he needed.

Except…Tammy?

Dammit, Henry needed Tammy.

No. He was holding Henry in his arms and Henry was at peace with his world. He was munching the note into a soggy pulp, his spare hand gripped his already battered teddy, and he was being held by a man in whom he had implicit trust.

Henry had everything he needed right here. Tammy was right. Somehow Henry had elected two grown-ups to be his people and Marc was one of them.

Henry was happy.

But Marc wasn't. Marc was feeling as if the world was closing in on him. All he'd tried to escape was right here, contentedly mulching paper. Ties. Family. Responsibility.

Love.

'I can care for you until breakfast, but not after that,' he said grimly, and Henry paused and thoughtfully tried to jam a piece of paper into Marc's mouth. 'No thanks, kid; I've had dinner.'

Undeterred, Henry went back to chewing.

'You need to go to bed.'

Did he? Henry looked unconvinced.

'I tell you what else you need…' There was a hint of sogginess under Marc's arm, and it didn't come from the paper. 'I guess your diapers will be up in Tammy's…I mean up in the nursery.'

The rooms were adjoining, Marc remembered. Tammy's bedroom was set up for a nanny. There was no door between it and the nursery. He'd take Henry up there, he decided, and if Tammy was still awake…

Surely she couldn't be asleep? Or if she happened to wake…

'Serve her right,' he decided. 'Who the heck does she think she is, trying to run my life? This is her job, not mine.'

She wasn't there.

Marc carried Henry into the nursery and just happened to glance—straight away—at the door to Tammy's bedroom. He'd expected a hump under the bedclothes. She'd pretend to be sleeping, he decided, and hadn't figured out whether to call her bluff and wake her or just leave Henry in the crib and let him wake her himself.

But she wasn't there!

Her bed was beautifully made up, as it had been since it was made by the servants that morning. It hadn't been slept in. The clothes she'd been wearing that night were lying on a bedside chair. Instinctively his eyes went to the wardrobe.

Hell! He couldn't help himself. In seconds he had the wardrobe door open, and when he saw her clothing still there he felt his breath escape in a sigh of relief.

She hadn't left the palace for good, then.

Why had he thought she would?

He hadn't, he told himself. He was just…checking.

So where was she?

'Tammy?'

No answer. Frustrated, he hit the servants' bell and listened to it echoing away in the distance. What had Tammy written?

> *As you tell me that I'm in charge, I've ordered the staff to bed.*

Where was she? Here he was, held close by Henry, when all he wanted to do was haul open the door and stride out into the night to find Tammy.

She'd be hidden in the servants' quarters, he decided. Or in any of the thirty or so empty bedchambers around the palace. Or out in the garden and up a tree. Anywhere.

Alone.

Damn.

Henry gave the beginning of a grumble of protest and the sogginess grew. He was going to have to cope with this crisis alone. He couldn't fetch Tammy even if he wanted to.

Damn, where was she?

Nowhere. He was by himself.

'This sort of thing isn't supposed to happen to royalty,' he told his cousin. 'I should head down to the servants' quarters and wake someone—rescind Tammy's orders— have someone else change you and look after you.'

Wouldn't that be what she'd expect him to do?

Yes.

She was expecting him to walk away. After all, that was just what he'd said he was going to do.

He closed his eyes and when he opened them he discovered Henry was watching him with wide-eyed wonder—as if he knew his future hung on what happened right this minute.

'I can change a diaper,' Marc said grimly, carrying Henry through to the change table. 'I can take care of a baby.'

He could.

But as he laid Henry down and tackled the first domestic duty it had ever fallen to him to undertake—as Henry beamed up at him in delight at the removal of something that had clearly been starting to irk him—Marc looked down into his little cousin's eyes and thought there was more to this than domestic duty. He wasn't just taking care of a baby.

He was falling in love!

The thought scared him so much that it took all the control he could muster not to walk out of the room right then. All he wanted was to take Henry down, knock on the housekeeper's bedroom door, hand over his responsibilities and run.

His responsibility gurgled up at him and smiled a fine baby smile, and the fine gossamer threads of responsibility tightened so firmly Marc thought he'd choke.

Instead, he somehow fastened a new diaper—in a fashion—lifted Henry into his arms and took him back to his suite.

And settled down to wonder where in hell Tammy was?

CHAPTER NINE

IT WAS a really long night.

Marc would have had to search hard if he'd tried to find Tammy because, instead of seeking out one of the scores of empty bedrooms in the palace and hoping Marc wouldn't find her, Tammy had escaped to where she belonged. He'd forgotten the standard gear that she always carried. A tent and a sleeping bag and the essentials to sleep under the stars. While Marc was struggling with diapers, Tammy was in her sleeping bag in her tent in the sheltered palace woodland.

But she wasn't asleep. She lay with the tent wide open, watching stars that were totally different from the galaxies she was used to in the Southern Hemisphere. Upside down and strange.

Being upside down made sense, she thought ruefully. Everything else was topsy-turvy. Why shouldn't the heavens match?

Why had she done this? What was she possibly hoping for?

A fair system of parenting, she told herself. But she knew it was far more than that. She wanted Marc to love his little cousin. She wanted Marc to…commit?

She wanted him to commit to Henry, she told herself savagely, and there was an aching void around her heart that she didn't understand. She didn't have a clue what to do with it.

Why had he kissed her?

She'd asked, 'What's changed?'

'You, of course,' he'd replied. 'You. And me.'

'It doesn't make sense,' she muttered, forcing herself to

remember her mother's words. 'The man's a womaniser.' So he kissed me. So what? If you breathe and you're female then you get kissed by His Royal Highness. I'm lucky it didn't go any further.

'Lucky?

'Yes, lucky.' She was talking out loud. She'd erected the tent well out of sight of the palace. Here she could conduct her conversation with herself without fear of interruption. Which was just as well. She had serious things to discuss.

'But if he'd wanted...

'To take things further? You're out of your mind, Tammy Dexter. He's just ditched Ingrid—in fact, you don't know for sure that he *has* ditched Ingrid. You want to fall into his arms between his little affairs with society bimbos?

'I wouldn't mind.

'Tamsin Dexter!' She was scolding herself, even managing to sound shocked, and she grinned into the night. Good grief. What on earth was happening to her?

She was fantasising over one gorgeous specimen of manhood. Maybe she'd been celibate for far too long. That was all this was. Fantasy.

So how was her fantastic male going with Henry?

'It's none of my business. Go to sleep.

'I could just sneak back and have a listen...

'Yeah, and get caught. You know darned well that would be the way of disaster.

'Why?

'Because...

'The servants will all be in bed. There'll just be Henry, who'll drift off to sleep pretty soon now. Which will leave me and His Highness, the Prince Regent.

'Not a good idea,' she told herself, zipping her sleeping bag up to her nose. 'In fact a very bad idea.'

So why did she desperately want to do it?

*   *   *

Where was she?

Henry's time clock was still out of kilter and he wanted to play, so Marc took his nephew back to bed, hauled open his laptop and started working on a design for a series of agricultural channels. He wasn't working very seriously. Henry's attention span was about thirty seconds, after which he demanded some new distraction. He'd come a long way from the baby who not a week before had known only that a window was the best distraction on offer.

Now Henry had found these wonderful new playthings called adults, and he intended to exploit them to the full. Teddy looked pretty boring compared to a clicking keyboard, and before long Marc's canal system looked like nothing so much as the work of a very drunken spider.

'So how are the farmers of Southern Broitenburg going to link up with this?' Marc demanded of his nephew, and Henry chortled, put his fist into the keyboard and sent a spiral of water channels veering northward.

'Oh, great. You realise you're sending water from a drought-affected area to one where the rainfall's the highest in Broitenburg?'

Henry clearly thought it was a great idea.

'Where's your aunt?'

Henry didn't know and he didn't care. Unlike Marc who found himself caring far too much.

'She came over here to look after you. That's her job.'

No comment.

'Damn, where is she?' He glanced at his watch. Two-thirty.

'She'd better be here in the morning.'

He didn't want her in the morning, he thought savagely. He wanted her now!

Tammy woke at dawn.

There was something about sleeping under the stars that

made waking at dawn almost compulsory—which was just as well. She didn't want to be found by the gardeners, so two minutes after waking she'd packed up and was returning to the palace.

She made herself slow. The servants would still be asleep. She'd ordered them not to stir before seven.

Maybe Marc would like a cup of tea, she thought dubiously, pausing in the front entrance, unsure what to do. If he'd been up all night with the baby…

If he'd been up all night the last thing he'd want now would be a cup of tea. He'd be fast asleep. She let herself into the kitchen, made herself tea and toast and kept on thinking about it.

Whether he'd like it or not, the temptation was irresistible.

'What man wouldn't want toast and tea at sunrise?' she asked herself, and she grinned. She knew the answer to that. 'But, hey, he deserves it. He's been working hard.'

The temptation was too much. She made him toast, loaded it with marmalade, and brewed fresh tea.

'Coming, ready or not,' she said, and took a deep breath.

What on earth was she doing?

She didn't have a clue.

He was dead to the world. They both were. Tammy's knock on the door to the main royal bedroom went unanswered. She pushed the vast door wide and saw them at once: one big prince and one little one, deeply lost in sleep.

Marc had been working when he'd fallen asleep. His laptop lay on the floor beside him, still powered up, fluorescent and flashing with something that looked like spiderwebs on the screen. Lines were scrawling everywhere. He'd fallen back on his pillows with the baby cradled to him.

Naked from the waist up, Marc's only covering was

Henry's already battered teddy. Henry himself lay cradled under his big cousin's arm, sound asleep and looking for all the world as if this was his very favourite place in the whole world.

Tammy stood, rooted to the spot, taking in the scene before her. She had a plate of toast in one hand and a mug of tea in the other, but she made no move to set them down. She couldn't.

The sight was enough to form a lump in her throat so large she could hardly swallow. She didn't know what on earth was happening to her, but the sight of this big man and this baby...

She didn't want relationships, she told herself fiercely. She wasn't interested in men. She should walk away fast— back out of this room right now. Instead she stood as if her eyes were locked on the sight before her.

Marc was so...large. His chest was tanned and strongly muscled. The tiny teddy sprawled over his breast accentuated the raw strength of the man.

Man and baby. They looked right together.

And the realisation slammed home. They belonged.

She didn't.

It was she who was the outsider. She'd come half a world to protect her small nephew but there'd been no need. If this man would protect him...love him...

She felt her eyes blur with tears.

Somehow she managed to back into the corridor, but the door hadn't swung shut behind her when Marc's eyes opened. For a long moment he stared at her, their eyes meeting across the room. Something passed between...

Good grief. She was so out of control. Her foot was holding the door open and she started shifting it. Still her eyes held his.

'Don't go.'

'I...'

He was out of the bed so fast she hardly saw him coming—lunging across the room to catch the door before it shut. Then he was steadying her, catching the toast, which was threatening to slide. He was right beside her. Right…there!

He was wearing only boxer shorts and nothing else. He was too large. He was too male. He was too darned much of anything you liked to name!

And she was so close to tears.

'Breakfast?' he asked, his dark eyes quizzing hers with easy laughter. 'You've brought me breakfast?'

'I thought…'

'You thought you should do something to make up for abandoning me last night?' he said dryly. 'How very kind.'

'I'm not being kind at all,' she managed, trying to make her voice indifferent. With no success at all. 'I just came to check on Henry.'

'Henry's fine.' Then his smile faded as he searched her face. His finger came up and touched her cheeks. It came away wet. 'Tears, Tammy?'

'No.' She gave her face an angry swipe. 'Why would I be crying?'

'I don't know.'

'I'm not.'

Still he searched.

'What is it?' he asked gently and the tears threatened to fall all over again.

'Nothing,' she managed, and hauled herself together. Somehow. 'I told you. I just wanted to check Henry.'

He gave her a long look, knowing he wasn't getting the whole truth but powerless to take it further. Finally he turned to the bed. Henry was snuggled into the pillows—a baby at peace with his world. 'Seeing as he's only been asleep for a couple of hours, I guess he might be fine a while longer.'

'He…he didn't go to sleep until late?'

'He didn't go to sleep until early.' Marc's laughter was back behind his eyes. 'Dawn was threatening to break, and so was I. Hell, Tam, I'm no babysitter.'

'I'm sorry.' The use of the diminutive of her name unnerved her still more, sneaking inside her defences so much she almost gave in right then. But then she thought about it and she knew.

They belonged together. More and more she knew it. Back in Australia she'd thought her relationship with Henry was the only one possible. Now she'd grown to realise that Marc needed his small cousin as much as Henry needed Marc. She'd fallen for Henry with every inch of her being, but loving him meant doing what was best for him.

Even if it meant her loss…

Marc was waiting for her to keep speaking. What had she said? That she was sorry? 'Actually, I'm not,' she corrected herself. 'I'm not sorry. Sleepless nights go with the territory of baby-care. It'll be my turn tonight.'

'Take him now.' Marc's smile was all embracing—pleading. He'd be able to get anything he ever wanted in life just by smiling like that, she thought bitterly. He lifted the mug from her and placed the tea and toast on the bedside table, then turned to smile that gorgeous smile at her from across the room. He was practically naked, she thought, a little bit desperately. Did he have any idea of the effect the sight of his body was having on her?

Apparently not. He'd moved on. 'You've made your point,' he told her. 'I've cared for him all night. Now take him back.'

But she was shaking her head. She had to stand her ground. She must. 'No.'

'What do you mean—no?'

'I mean it's a twenty-four-hour thing,' she told him. 'You

take his care for twenty-four hours. Then it's my turn. I come on duty at dinner tonight.'

'But…'

'But what?'

He sighed and ran his fingers through his thatch of dark hair. 'I can always get Mrs Burchett to take care of him.'

'Of course you can,' she said coldly. 'That's a royal thing, after all. Hand over your responsibility to the servants.'

'He's not my responsibility.'

'Whose responsibility is he, then?'

That was easy. 'Yours.'

'No.' She shook her head. 'I'm here to make sure Henry's cared for and loved. I'm not here to take on his full-time care. I'm not here waiting for you to palm off your responsibilities.'

'I am not palming—'

'Yes, you are.' Somehow she managed a smile. 'So there. I've delivered your breakfast and my job here is done.'

'Your job?' He glared. 'You sound like Superman, who's just saved the world as we know it. What do you mean, your job here is done?'

'Toast and marmalade.' She grinned again. 'Not quite saving the world, but close.' She had to get out of there. Now! 'I'm glad you're getting on so well,' she told him. 'Have a happy day. Leave Henry with Mrs Burchett if you must.' Tammy knew enough of Mrs Burchett to realise that Henry would be very well cared for in that elderly lady's arms. 'But you must realise that he's bonded to *you*.'

'Tammy…'

'I'm off to care for some trees,' she told him, and kept right on determinedly smiling. 'That's my career.' She motioned to the laptop on the floor. 'Like yours. By the way, that looks like a really interesting irrigation system. I may not be too good at geography, but that water seems to be running *up* the mountains. Well done, you. What an engineer!'

And before he could say another word she turned and fled, leaving him staring after her, as stunned as he'd ever been in his life.

Marc ate his toast and drank his tea and watched Tammy's slim figure through the window as she made her way back down the south lawn to the woodland beyond. She was carrying what looked from here to be a chainsaw. It was too big for such a slight girl, he thought, and then he thought of Ingrid carrying a chainsaw. He found himself wincing. The image was too ridiculous.

Tammy looked free and happy and intent on the task at hand. She didn't look like someone who'd dumped a baby on him for effect. She truly looked as if she wasn't going to spare a thought for him all day.

He wasn't accustomed to women treating him like this, he decided. Women with chainsaws. Women who dumped babies on him.

Women who made him smile.

He wasn't accustomed to women like Tammy.

Maybe there *were* no women like Tammy. She disappeared behind a beech grove and he felt her departure like a physical wrench.

Maybe he could wander down there some time today and see what she was doing.

No. He was going home today. He was leaving!

Or was he?

Beside him Henry slept on, blissfully unaware of the tension in the adult world. And why not? Henry was being cared for and played with and loved for the first time in his small life. Marc put a hand down to touch his tiny fingers and involuntarily Henry's small hand curled around his.

There was a clenching in his chest that was so sudden and so savage it was as if someone had kicked him.

He was supposed to be leaving! Today!

He *could* hand Henry over to Mrs Burchett, he thought desperately. Madge would love him to bits. Henry would be fine with Madge.

But Henry hadn't bonded to Madge. He'd bonded to him. To Marc.

He did not want this!

What did he want?

Tammy.

Hell, and that was the way of madness.

He should go back to sleep, he thought. He'd only had two hours' sleep. There was no reason to get up.

But Tammy was somewhere down in the woods, playing with a chainsaw.

He wasn't going near Tammy. He was going home.

Yeah, right. He glanced down again at the linking of his large hand with the tiny one of his little cousin and he knew he was doing no such thing. He'd stay here today. He wouldn't go near Tammy, though. Hell, a man had some pride and if she thought...

She thought nothing. She wanted nothing from him. She didn't dress to attract. He'd seen her dressed to kill, but that had only been to stop Ingrid treating her as a poor relation. When Marc was around she didn't care what she wore.

Had she even noticed that he was a man?

Of course she had. When he'd kissed her she'd kissed him right back.

The memory of those kisses was enough to make him groan and shove a pillow over his head. Hell, he didn't respond like that to women. He didn't.

He'd care for Henry today, and at dinner tonight he'd have it out with Tammy. They had to sort out some sort of sensible arrangement. She must agree to take on Henry's permanent care.

He had to get out of here before he went nuts.

The day seemed endless. More than once Marc looked longingly at the housekeeping bell, but something held him back. Maybe it was the way Henry clung to him. Maybe it was the way the baby chortled when he tried to make him laugh, or maybe it was the thought of Tammy's scorn if she returned to the house and found Henry handed over to the servants.

It wasn't just Tammy, he conceded as the day wore on. It was the thought of Henry's distress. The baby had somehow crept around his heart, and he didn't have a clue what to do with how he was feeling.

He'd care for Henry today, but tonight he'd hand him over to Tammy and escape, he thought. Immediately! The way he figured it, if this was how he felt then Tammy must feel the same. He'd call her bluff. If he found it hard to dump Henry with the servants, then Tammy would find it impossible.

All it needed was his departure. So…he'd stick around until dinnertime tonight and then he'd go.

It was a really long day.

Tammy didn't return to the house for lunch. She'd taken a packed lunch, Mrs Burchett told him, and the compulsion to carry Henry down through the beech grove to see what she was doing became almost overwhelming.

He did take Henry outdoors. The baby loved the garden, and to his own astonishment Marc found himself wandering round talking to the little boy as if he could really understand.

'This is what you'll inherit one day, Henry. Your responsibility. And your pleasure.'

And there *was* pleasure, he discovered. He'd always found this place oppressive, but today it was somehow different. The lakes and formal gardens, and beyond them the acres and acres of woodland, looked different. He found he was looking at it with Tammy's eyes and finding it wonderful.

Tammy would do wonders with this place.

His steps turned involuntarily towards the beech grove. 'Your Aunty Tammy is just through here...'

But he stopped himself—somehow. They'd lead different lives, Tammy had decreed, and he could only agree with her. He must.

So instead of taking Henry to see his aunty wielding a chainsaw he forced his steps back to the house. A couple of storybooks later and a good dinner and Henry was asleep. Finally.

Maybe he could leave now.

It was five o'clock. Henry was deeply asleep. Tammy had agreed to take over his care from seven o'clock, and it'd be a miracle if Henry woke before then. Mrs Burchett could easily and safely keep an eye on him. He could just walk out the door right now and drive away and that would be that.

But his laptop was still set up with his work on it, and it was sort of easier just to sit next to his big bed where Henry lay sleeping and make plans for a proper irrigation system— one where the pipes didn't go up the mountain—and keep an eye on Henry as well. After all, if he woke...

Or he could just watch him and think about Tammy...

And then it was too late. 'Dinner's in ten minutes,' Dominic told him. 'Miss Tammy's in the front salon. I've lit the fire.'

It sounded really good to him, and walking away now would be boorish. Wouldn't it?

*   *   *

Tammy was in jeans.

Marc had dressed as he normally dressed for dinner in any of the royal residences—in a dark suit and tie—and her appearance by the fire set him aback. Maybe he'd grown accustomed to her in her sister's gorgeous dresses. The jeans she was wearing were clean and fresh, but still they jarred.

'I'm not a princess,' she said, jutting her chin as he paused in the doorway and he thought, How the hell did she know what I was thinking?

'I beg your pardon?'

'You were thinking I should have dressed appropriately. I have.'

'I don't know what you're talking about.'

'I think you do.' She was eyeing him cautiously, noting the dark shadows under his eyes. 'You didn't go back to sleep, huh?'

He was thrown completely off balance. 'After you left…?'

'You need to sleep when you can with babies,' she advised him kindly. 'You can catch up tomorrow, but after that you might like to readjust your schedule.'

'Look, Tammy—'

'Shall we eat?'

'No!' It was almost an expletive. He crossed the three steps between them and gripped her shoulders, forcing her to meet his eyes. He had to make her see. 'This plan of yours is crazy.'

'Why is it crazy?' Maybe he'd intended her to be thrown off balance by his nearness—by his gripping her like this— but the gaze that met his was direct and clear. 'It's the only possible plan in the circumstances.'

'You came here to care for your nephew.'

'I told you exactly why I came,' she retorted. 'I came to see that he's loved and well looked after. You love him. You can look after him.'

'I don't love him.'

'Don't you?' She smiled then, her eyes crinkling at the edges in a way he was starting to really, really like. 'Maybe you don't,' she agreed cordially. 'Yet. But I've seen his response to you and I've seen that you can't bear for him to suffer. I might not have been near the palace today but I have my spies.'

'What the hell—?'

'I've had progress reports all day.' It was as if he was across the room from her. She seemed completely unaware that he was still gripping her. 'The staff told me about every move you made. You couldn't bear to let him be, even when he was asleep.'

'I don't—'

'You don't do love?' she said thoughtfully. 'So you say. So everyone says. You're a womaniser who goes from one relationship to another. But Henry's not like that. Henry's not a woman you can walk away from. Marc, you've never let yourself love anyone since your mother died, and here's Henry about to cure you in a way that you never imagined possible.'

Her reply left him speechless. Almost. 'For God's sake,' he told her, 'when will you get it into your thick head that I don't want to be cured?'

'You don't want to be loved?'

'No!'

'And you don't think that maybe you've fallen head over heels in love with your little cousin?'

'No!'

'Liar.'

They were inches apart now. Her colour was heightened but still she met his gaze, unflinching. 'I'm not going to let you walk away from this, you know,' she told him. 'Not now. I reared my sister practically single-handed and she broke my heart at the end of it. If you leave me in sole charge of Henry the same thing could happen again. But I'm not going to let it. I need help, and you're it.'

'You're afraid.' He said it with a note of discovery in his voice and saw her flinch. But still she met his eyes.

'Yes,' she agreed, with only a hint of a tremor in her voice. 'Yes, I am. But at least I acknowledge it and I'm doing something about it.'

'By coercing me…'

'No one's coercing you but your own heart. You could have walked away from Henry today and left him with Mrs Burchett. What held you back?'

'You,' he said explosively, and saw that damned smile peep out again.

'What? Me?'

'You are the most infuriating woman…the rudest, push-iest, mostly badly dressed…'

'Hey!'

'What?'

'I'm not badly dressed. I'm dressed just fine for where I belong. Which isn't here.'

'You belong here.'

'No.'

'You do,' he told her, goaded beyond endurance. 'You think just because you speak in that damned Australian accent and swing from trees and carry chainsaws…'

'That I can't be royalty? Then I'd be right.'

'You'd be wrong.'

'If you want a princess bring back Ingrid. She's aching—'

'Damn Ingrid!'

'Why on earth,' she said slowly—thoughtfully, even—'would I want to damn Ingrid?'

Silence. The tension in the room was almost unbearable. It was way past serving time, but Dominic was standing on the other side of the oak doors and he wasn't entering for worlds. It was far below his dignified standing as royal butler to put his ear against the door, but he did have to wait for a pause in the conversation after all—and if his ear happened to be perilously close...

There was nothing to hear any more. Tammy was gazing up at Marc, her eyes bright with tension and the traces of anger clearly written on her face. And Marc was staring down at her, goaded beyond bearing.

Why would she want to damn Ingrid?

For no reason at all, he thought savagely. Ingrid didn't come into the equation.

Her eyes were still watching him, bright with enquiry. His hands still gripped her shoulders and held, and she didn't pull away. Why should she?

Why should she indeed?

And the fine line beyond forbearance and fury was broken. He was only human after all. He was a man...

Once more he pulled her into his arms and kissed her.

CHAPTER TEN

THE line between hate and love was a fine one. If Marc had been asked that morning whether he did either he would have laughed. But now...

He was so out of control he hardly knew what he was doing, and when he hauled her close, when his mouth bent and took hers, it was furious, blind, irrational rage that was pushing him.

It was rage.

Of course it was rage. He wanted to punish her. He wanted to make her see how impossible she was. How impossible her being here was. How crazy was the way he was feeling—that he wanted her—that he ached for her—that his body was screaming in a way he didn't recognise. When she smiled at him his gut twisted in a savage, searing pain. The scent of her... Her nearness... She was like a lovely creature just out of his reach.

She was so desirable.

Why didn't she fight him? he wondered in that tiny part of his brain that was capable of such thought. She should kick him and run.

Maybe *she* should leave. She had no place here. She belonged half a world away, her nephew belonged here with the servants, and he belonged in his own château...

No. Nothing was what it seemed. Nothing was happening as it should. His world had tipped and was refusing to right itself. All he knew was the way she felt in his hands—the way her breasts moulded to his chest—the way he wanted her...

He wanted her!

Her lips were opening under his, a rose unfurling from bud, and it was no longer anger he was feeling. The fury was surging out of him to be replaced by an emotion that was even stronger.

He mustn't!

Dear God, this woman…

She was so sweet. She was so lovely. Her mouth was yielding to his and her hands were clinging to him.

How could she respond? How could she possibly feel what he felt? This yearning, tearing pull…

All his life he'd avoided this, and here, under his hands, was the thing he'd tried so desperately to escape. She was his woman. His! Half of his whole. He'd never known he was incomplete, and yet she fitted to him as though he'd been torn in half at birth and not known. Until now, when she melted with such searing sweetness…

He couldn't move. He could only hold her and kiss her and feel the surge of change rip his whole being.

Tammy…

And Tammy?

Like Marc she was powerless to stop even if she'd wanted to. Which she didn't.

How could she stop? She'd never thought anything could be so sweet—so right.

Oh, Marc was all wrong for her. In the sane part of her mind she knew it. But for this moment she knew nothing. There was a whole gamut of emotions surging and she had nothing to compare them with. She felt as if she was surging into another life though the medium of this man's body.

What had Shakespeare said? '*A consummation devoutly to be wished.*'

A consummation.

That was what this was, she thought dazedly. A consummation. Whether they took it further than this or not made no difference. She was merging into him right now—changing—learning that there was a whole sweet world that had been locked to her until now.

He was a womaniser. That was what her mother called him. Mrs Burchett agreed and she'd seen nothing to dispel the idea. Tomorrow he'd move on. Tomorrow he would no longer hold her like this—not kiss her as he was kissing her. Tomorrow he'd make no claim on her, nor she on him. She knew that.

Tomorrow…tomorrow was for the whole barren future.

But for now there was only him. The feel of him. The wonder. The aching need.

So her lips welcomed him, her hands clung and she felt her body light with fire. He was her man. For this sweet time—for this minute, maybe, if that was all there was—he was her home.

Marc…

'Marc.'

Somehow she whispered his name. Somehow he drew back, to take a breath and devour her with his eyes before bending his mouth again to hers.

'Marc.'

It made him pause. The way she whispered it was a caress in itself, and its sweetness threatened to overwhelm him. Her sweetness…her tenderness…

This wasn't a woman playing on his terms, he thought dazedly. Women like Ingrid—they understood the rules. They used men and were used by them in turn. He needed a society hostess and a partner and they wanted status. When they became too pushy he moved on, but there were no broken hearts. He partnered experienced women who played the game as he expected.

But there was no game here.

He gazed down into Tammy's eyes and saw something he'd never seen. She was gazing up at him with all the tenderness in the world. She was giving…

And he knew. If he lifted her triumphantly now and carried her up the wide staircase to his bedchamber she'd give herself with all the joy in her heart.

She'd give herself to him.

Dear God…

For a long time he gazed down into her eyes. She was looking back at him, a half-smile on her lips and her eyes wide and questioning. Teasing, almost… Waiting.

Waiting for commitment?

No. Waiting for whatever he was prepared to give, because the commitment was already there. He could read it in her eyes. They were shining up at him. Her lips were still slightly parted with an invitation that was almost irresistible. She was waiting.

All he had to do was gather her to him and she was his—for however long he wanted her.

He did want her, he thought with a desperate savagery. He wanted her more than he'd wanted anything in his life. But how could he take her and then put her away from him?

He couldn't. If he took her now…

If he took her now he took her for ever. And he couldn't do it.

He didn't love.

Or maybe he did.

She was watching him, still with that faint questioning smile, as if she sensed that he was battling with himself. Maybe he knew that here was a woman who'd love him. Who'd give herself to him as she'd given herself to her little nephew. She'd dropped everything and come to the other side of the world. For love.

He had no right to accept a love like that. He was flawed. Hell, his whole damned family was flawed. This place—royalty—was a goldfish bowl. To bring a woman into it—a woman of such innocence—to bind her so that she could never leave…

That was what was being offered here, he thought. She was offering herself. She was offering the devotion his mother had given his father.

A devotion that destroyed.

'I can't.'

It was a groan, and the smile on Tammy's face wavered and died.

'You can't?'

'I can't do this, Tammy,' he told her. 'I'm not... I don't...'

What was he saying? Her brow furrowed, two tiny lines creasing between her eyes. 'Marc, I'm not asking...'

'You're not asking anything,' he said savagely. 'You don't. You give and you give and you give. Well, damn, I'm not taking. I'm not destroying this.'

'I don't know what you mean.'

'You're beautiful,' he told her. Somehow he broke away and took two blind steps backward. 'You're the most beautiful woman I've ever met. You're wonderful to the core and I'm damned if I'm hauling you into this mess.'

She tilted her head to one side and the creases between her eyes stayed. 'I'm sorry?'

'Royalty.'

'I think I already am embroiled in this mess,' she said candidly. 'Up to my eyebrows.'

'And if I take you...? If you and I...?'

'It wouldn't just be you doing the taking,' she said softly. 'I'm a big girl, Your Highness, and I know what I want.' The smile came back again—the teasing mischief that made his heart wrench within him. 'I want you.'

How was he supposed to answer that? One way, his body screamed at him. One way. Lunge back and take her in his arms and carry her up...

No! He was so far out of control he didn't know what he

was doing. He didn't. Hell, where was he supposed to take this?

He was doing harm. He was in danger of causing this bright innocence to be destroyed.

He had to get away.

'I…I need to leave,' he managed, and her smile died again.

'Tomorrow?'

'No.' He closed his eyes, and when he opened them the way was clear to him. 'I'm sorry, Tammy, I need to leave right now. Forgive me.'

'But…'

'I'm sorry,' he said again, and wrenched away to open the door so suddenly that Dominic, standing not so innocently on the other side, nearly fell over. Marc didn't even notice. 'Give Miss Dexter her dinner,' he told the butler. 'I'm not eating here tonight. Look after Tammy for me, will you, Dominic?'

And without another word he took the stairs two at a time and disappeared.

How was a girl supposed to eat after that?

Tammy made a dreary figure, sitting in solitary state at the splendid dining table. Dominic served her in silence, all the time watching out of the corners of his wise old eyes but not saying a word. She was white-faced and silent herself, and he knew without being told that she didn't require dessert or coffee. As he helped her to rise they heard the unmistakeable sound of Marc's car disappearing down the long, long driveway.

If anything Tammy's face grew even whiter, and Dominic placed his hand on her arm in an unconscious gesture of support.

'Thank you.' Her voice was bleak. 'I'm…I'm sorry I've

made a bad fist of dinner. It was delicious. Will you tell the kitchen staff...?'

'That it was despite their cooking—not because of it—that you couldn't eat,' he said gently. 'Yes, miss. We understand.'

'Will he come back, do you think?' she asked, and he turned to look at the disappearing lights of Marc's car.

'Not without your encouragement,' he told her, and she blinked.

'I don't know what you mean.'

'You don't know how to encourage him? No, miss.' He looked at her for a long minute and then sighed, unconsciously bracing. He needed to talk to this chit of a girl. It wasn't his place, but maybe the future of the principality depended on it. 'You understand he's running scared?'

She stared. 'I don't understand.'

There was a long hesitation, as if Dominic was having second thoughts—which indeed he was—and then he shrugged. He liked this wan-faced girl. All the servants did. She'd been here only a couple of days, yet already the place was starting to feel like home—as it hadn't for years.

'What do you think would happen if Master Henry wasn't here?' he asked, and Tammy frowned.

'Marc told me. He said the country would lose its royal family.'

Dominic shook his head. 'That's not quite true. The crown would pass to Prince Marc.'

Tammy frowned. 'But...Marc said if Henry didn't inherit then the monarchy would die.'

'Only because Prince Marc would refuse to accept the crown. He feels he has no choice. He hates this family and everything it represents.'

The butler shrugged again, clearly deciding to go the whole way. This was no way for a butler to behave, but Dominic was much more than a butler. In Tammy he glimpsed salvation for his country, and if that involved indiscretion on his part then so be it.

'Marc's father had an affair with his uncle's wife with disastrous consequences,' he said softly. 'His mother committed suicide because of it. Then there was a girl Marc was involved with. It was some years ago now, but Marc thought he was in love. Being third in line to the throne, he needed his uncle's consent in order to marry, so he brought her here. Franz, the older of his two cousins, took one look and decided he'd have her for himself. The prospect of the crown was so enticing that Marc was summarily dumped.'

'Oh, no.'

'Indeed, miss,' the butler said dourly. 'And I'm afraid it grew worse. Franz used her for his own ends but he had no intention of marrying her. She ended up pregnant and alone. She died of drug abuse and we still have no clear answer whether it was suicide or accident.'

'I…see.' Tammy did see, and she was appalled. The vision of a much younger Marc, betrayed, scorned, and then having to live with such a consequence, was dreadful. Oh, Marc…

But there was more Dominic needed to tell her. 'I wonder whether you do see, miss?' he said softly, his eyes on her face. 'Every contact Marc ever had with this place turned to poison. When Franz died and Jean-Paul was killed—both incidents that cemented Marc's disgust of the place—he was landed with the prospect of inheriting what was for him a tainted crown. The only way to escape it was to bring Henry back fast enough to inherit.'

'So he lied to me,' Tammy said, frowning. 'He said…'

'I believe he said if Henry didn't inherit then no one could,' the butler told her. 'It's what he believes himself, because he knows he couldn't bear to inherit. He can hardly bear to step into this palace, much less inherit the crown.'

'But if I took Henry home…'

'Back to Australia?' The butler was watching her and Tammy didn't know what he was thinking. How could he see what was in her heart? He certainly seemed to. 'If you did that then you'd be forcing Marc to inherit,' he told her. 'He's said he couldn't, but if it came to the crunch I believe he would take up his responsibility. He loves his country. He loves his people. It's this palace he hates.'

'It's not this palace,' Tammy said strongly. 'This palace is beautiful. It's the people in his past who are dreadful. People who are dead.'

'Yes, miss. But how can we teach him that?'

They stared at each other—elderly retainer and young woman—and Tammy saw a reflection of her own fear in the old man's face.

'You love him,' she said on a note of discovery, and Dominic nodded.

'Yes, miss,' he said simply. 'I've always worked for his family. Master Marc—I mean His Royal Highness—brought me here after Jean-Paul died to try to clear up the mess that this place was in. I cared for him when he was a tiny boy. I put him on his first pony and I've watched him grow. I helped bury his mother and it was me who gave him the news that his ex-fiancée had died. It makes me feel ill to see him suffer again now.'

'Suffer...'

'I believe he loves you,' Dominic said gently. 'That's why I'm talking to you like this. It's not my business, but I can see what's happening.'

'He loves me?' She was staring at the butler as if he'd lost his mind.

But Dominic's voice was sure. 'Yes, miss.'

'He hardly knows me.'

'He knows you.' Dominic smiled, a smile of infinite sadness. 'So do we all.'

'But...' She flinched, trying to take this on board. She

couldn't. Marc? Love her? The thing was impossible. He had so many women.

'Why do you think he's left now?' Dominic asked her, and Tammy tried to make her confused mind focus. But all she could see was one clear path—right back to Australia.

'I can't stay here,' she said on a note of finality. 'I can't. I...'

'You love him, too.'

'No. *Yes*. I don't know!' She turned to stare out of the vast French windows, as if she could still see Marc's disappearing car. 'This is impossible. If I took Henry back to Australia then Marc would inherit, like it or not. He'd be forced to take on his responsibilities.'

'But he'd never learn to love,' Dominic told her and she turned back to him, her eyes bright with unshed tears.

'What on earth am I meant to do about that?'

There was no answer. They both knew it. Nothing. What was there to be done?

'Hell.' It was a whisper of fear. 'Oh, Dominic...'

'Yes, miss,' Dominic said simply. He opened the door and stood aside while she passed out into the corridor. His confidences were clearly at an end. 'It is hell. I don't know what to do about it, and neither does anyone here. We're hoping for a miracle, and only you can provide it.'

She didn't get much sleep that night. After waking and playing until midnight Henry decided to revert to European time and snooze like an angel until morning. Not so his aunt. She paced the bedroom, tried unsuccessfully to sleep, and then paced some more.

What could she do?

Leave? Take Henry back to Australia? To a lifetime of childcare and single parenthood?

Would he hate her for robbing him of the throne? Maybe he would. And Marc would be left here—alone.

Could she stay here? Share Henry's care with Marc? See him every other day? Hope Dominic was right?

Dominic couldn't be right. How could such a man as Marc love her?

There was no sleep at all.

The following day she did some haphazard work in the gardens during Henry's afternoon nap. But for the rest of the time she played with him, talked with him, and tried to keep her mind off what was happening to his big cousin.

Her love.

She loved him. The knowledge was now seared into her heart with a clarity that was blinding. She'd fallen in love with her little nephew and then she'd fallen even more deeply in love with his big cousin.

The whole situation was impossible. Absurd. She didn't belong. Marc himself should be living here. He was either Prince Regent or Crown Prince, depending on what she did.

She could take Henry back to Australia and Marc would be Crown Prince, like it or not. A lonely Crown Prince. A man alone with his shadows. Or she could stay here with Henry and watch Marc be Prince Regent, independent and aloof.

And she'd go quietly nuts.

As the day wore on she hugged her little nephew over and over again, until she was sure he'd object, but he simply cooed at her and tried to pull her hair, and her heart twisted and twisted until she thought it would tear apart.

Because there was one more choice, and as the day wore on she saw that it was the only choice she could make. But it was the hardest decision she'd made in her life. How could she do it?

How could she not?

It was seven at night. Marc was at his desk in the huge front room he'd used as his study ever since he'd inherited

Renouys. It was a magnificent room, furnished more for comfort than for style, and it was here that he considered himself home.

Not in that other place, he thought bitterly as he stared unseeing at the work in front of him. Not in the royal palace. His own home was grand enough, but it wasn't a whisker on the Broitenburg royal residence.

The Broitenburg palace was Henry's home, he told himself. And Tammy's. It was no place for him. He'd done his duty for his country. He'd brought his tiny cousin home. If Tammy... No, if *Henry* needed him then he was available for the short time his assistance was required, but this was where he belonged.

So why did it seem so bleak? Why did this place that had always seemed such a sanctuary suddenly seem so empty?

He should contact his friends, he thought. Not Ingrid. He'd moved on from Ingrid. Other friends. He had a brilliant social circle. All he had to do was lift the phone and he'd have people down here. Or he could drive up to the city— catch up with friends at their home base. See a few shows. Try out the new restaurant everyone was talking about.

It held no appeal at all.

He had work to do. He clicked his computer mouse and a design sprang to life. It was the design Henry had 'helped' him with two nights before.

Water still flowing uphill? Hmm. Maybe it needed a little more work.

But, instead of starting to correct things, he found himself staring down at the screen and smiling. Hell, he'd enjoyed playing with Henry so much.

He'd still see him.

He shook himself, realising where his thoughts were taking him. Right back to Tammy!

Sure, he'd see Henry, but from now on he'd see him on

his terms, he thought savagely. Not on the crazy terms Tammy had set. Every second day...

Ridiculous.

He glanced at his watch. Seven. Ha! On Tammy's terms he'd be taking over Henry's care right now. Well, he'd sorted that out. She'd be back at the palace and she'd settle down to care for Henry and her precious trees. Alone.

Which was what he wanted—wasn't it?

Of course it was. Tammy had nothing to do with him. So he had no right to be feeling as he was feeling right now. As if she'd just drive up the driveway and open the door and come into his arms...

Crazy. It was a crazy way to think and he had to move on. He and Tammy? No and no and no.

He had to do some work! He turned back to his laptop but was distracted by the sound of a car approaching. He half rose and then settled. It'd be nothing, he told himself, annoyed that his gut had given a stupid, hopeful lurch. It'd be a tradesman. A delivery van. This was a working farm, after all, and he had a farm manager who'd see to things.

He needed to do some work.

But there were voices, muted in the distance, and he found himself pausing so that he could listen without the distraction of a clicking keyboard. There was a soft murmur and a man's voice responding. André. His farm manager.

'Over there, miss. Straight through the front door and first turn to the left.'

He froze.

Tammy.

She had to do this. She had to say what she needed to say and get out of here. She had to keep her face in order—not cry—not hold onto Henry a moment longer than she needed to.

How? She was breaking her heart. She couldn't believe

she was doing this. That she'd come to this dreadful decision...

She didn't know, but somehow she had to do it.

She didn't belong here. Henry belonged here and so did Marc.

Let the two of them get on with it.

'Tammy.'

Marc had risen and was out of the study and into the hall before she'd entered the room. At the sight of her he stopped dead.

'Marc.' Her tone was cool and careful. She was wearing her customary jeans, T-shirt and battered sneakers and he thought, How the hell had he ever thought someone like Ingrid could be beautiful? Could clothes and grooming make someone beautiful? The thought was a farce.

She was just...lovely.

But Tammy was carrying Henry and she wasn't thinking of her appearance. Her eyes were frozen.

There was pain behind her gaze, he thought. Why?

Tammy's voice, when she spoke again, was rigidly formal.

'It's time,' she said blankly, and before he knew what she was about she'd walked forward and placed Henry into his arms. The little boy was delighted to see him. He chuckled and tried to grab a fistful of Marc's dark hair. Marc let him pull. His eyes were on only Tammy.

'What are you doing?' She'd set a bag containing baby things down on the floor. Now she was eyeing him from six feet away and the pain behind her eyes was unmistakeable. Was that a glimmer of tears?

'I told you; this is not my job,' she said, in a voice that wasn't quite steady. 'My role is to see that Henry is cared for and loved. With you I know that he will be.'

'But...'

'I didn't come here to be Henry's full-time carer. He loves you as well as me.'

'But I don't…'

'Love him? You do, you know.' Her face was totally expressionless now, as if she was holding herself rigidly under control. 'You're capable of all the love in the world, but you won't let yourself see it. You're afraid. Well, that's okay with me—I can wear it—but Henry can't. Henry needs you, and you need him. You need each other whether you intend to be Prince Regent or Crown Prince. Either way. Take your pick.'

He felt as if he'd been punched. Hard. 'How do you know…?'

'I'm not blind,' she said shortly. 'You're running scared, Marc. Well, I have been too, but something's happened. What's between you and me…it's made me see that the world's what we make it. I'm afraid I've fallen in love with you, Marc.' Then, as he made an involuntary protest, she shook her head. 'No. I shouldn't have said that. It's not fair to lay my weakness on you. I'm not expecting you to do anything with it. Why would I? I've lived a long time without any sort of loving and I know I can keep on that way. So can you, I guess. But Henry's the one who's important. He's a very special little boy. He needs a daddy. He needs you, Marc, and I won't let you walk away from that need.'

'So you're leaving him here?' Marc said blankly. He wasn't too sure what was happening here. What she was saying was leaving him stunned, and it didn't explain the look of blank misery on her face. Or did it? 'You're leaving him here until tomorrow night?'

'I'm leaving him here until he needs me,' she said bluntly, and turned on her heel and ran down the steps before he could say a word.

Before he could see the tears streaming down her face. Tears of goodbye.

*   *   *

What had she said?

I'm afraid I've fallen in love with you…

He stood staring out at her retreating back and thought he must have been hearing things. How the hell could she decide she loved him? She'd known him for so short a time.

Didn't she know he could destroy her? His family—the royal connection—it contaminated all it touched.

Did he love Tammy?

No! He didn't love anyone. He didn't *do* love!

But Henry was in his arms, gurgling up at him, making him rethink everything he'd believed in for so long.

Making him rethink love?

It was impossible, he decided fiercely. Put it away. Think about the arrangements Tammy was trying to force on him. Twenty-four hours of turnabout childcare… How could this work?

It was farcical, Marc decided, but he gave the little boy his supper and tried desperately not to think about the stricken look on Tammy's face or the reason behind it. How could they juggle the baby back and forth between two households? A day here—a day there?

Maybe Tammy was right. Maybe he *should* go back to live in the palace with Tammy and Henry on a permanent basis.

No! It was impossible. It made a mockery of all he'd spent his life achieving.

Independence. Sanity.

And the love thing…

No. He didn't want to go there. He'd kissed her once too often. He'd been a fool to do it and somehow he'd have to undo the damage.

'Your aunt hasn't got the sense to see how impossible this is,' Marc told Henry, and Henry gurgled and grinned and demanded another toast finger. 'She'll have to take you full time. Maybe I can take you at weekends. Sometimes.'

But even that was too much. The longer he spent with Henry the more the little boy wormed his way into his heart.

He'd leave him with the servants.

No. He couldn't do it and Tammy knew he couldn't. This was emotional blackmail, he thought furiously, and then thought— What had he tried to use with her? He'd tried to offload his responsibilities onto her slender shoulders and maybe it wasn't fair.

'I'll take you home tomorrow night and make her see reason,' he told Henry, and had a toast finger land on his nose in response. 'Gee, thanks. Maybe your aunt can teach you table manners.'

But...

She...loved him?

He hadn't imagined what she'd said. Her words kept ringing over and over in his brain but he shoved them away with all the force he could muster. They didn't make sense. She hadn't meant them. Or, if she had, well, then she just had to get over it.

He didn't do love.

Then Henry dropped his toast, and the ancient collie who always slept by the stove leapt to his feet like a pup of six months and devoured it in a gulp. Henry's roar of indignation almost raised the roof, and he sobbed inconsolably into Marc's shoulder.

He didn't do relationships?

'We'll make some more toast,' he told Henry, then wiped the little boy's eyes and gave him a shame-faced grin. 'Okay, I know I'm hooked. I'm hooked on you. But it's only for today. After that...somehow I'll get my distance back, and that's the way I'll keep it.'

*   *   *

He wanted distance? Unbeknownst to Marc, that was exactly what he was getting.

Half an hour after Henry had demolished his last toast finger—while Marc racked his brains for a bedtime story to encourage his little cousin to sleep—half an hour after that Tammy was boarding a plane headed for Australia.

'What do you mean, she's gone?'

'She left for Australia last night.' Dominic glanced at his watch. 'I imagine she's nearly in Sydney by now.'

'She can't have.' It was seven p.m. Time for handover. Marc had driven Henry back to the palace thinking this was the end. He'd make it clear to Tammy that from now on Henry was hers. But now he was standing at the castle entrance with a sleepy Henry in his arms while he stared at the elderly butler in bewilderment.

He and Henry had had a truly excellent day. Aware that this was the last day he'd agree to have him, Marc had shelved work and given himself up to amuse his tiny cousin. Now, almost asleep, Henry twined his little arms around Marc's neck and snuggled into Marc's shoulder. The butler gave the baby a curious glance as he responded to Marc's demand.

'I'm sorry, sir, but that's just what she has done. She had her things in the car when she dropped Master Henry off to you last night, and went straight on to the airport.'

'You knew she was leaving?'

'Yes, sir.'

Marc was staring at him as if he'd lost his mind. 'You didn't tell me? You didn't contact me?'

'Miss Tammy asked us not to, and we couldn't see the need.'

'You couldn't see the need!'

'No, sir.'

'But…' He shook his head. Tammy, on a plane. Tammy, returning to Australia. Without him!

The thought made him feel ill. But Dominic was watching him with a strange expression on his face and somehow he forced himself back to practicalities. To things that mattered.

Tammy leaving…

Henry. Think of Henry.

'She's supposed to be looking after Henry.'

'Yes, sir.'

'So who's supposed to be looking after him now?'

'I believe Miss Tammy assumed you would, sir,' Dominic said woodenly, and Marc cast him a sudden suspicious look.

'You're in on this!'

'I afraid I don't know what you mean, sir.' The butler's face was impassive—which meant that Marc was even more certain.

'It's a plot!'

The butler's mouth twitched. 'Are you going to drag me out at dawn and have me shot?'

'I should.' Marc eyed him with frustrated bewilderment. 'Damn, I should. What the hell's going on, Dom?'

Dominic's face relaxed a little, his old eyes creasing in sympathy. 'I believe Miss Tammy meant this for the best,' he said simply. 'Would you like to read her note?'

'She left a note?'

'Yes, sir.'

Marc took a deep breath. Then he carefully set Henry on the polished wood floor, gave him his shoelace to untie and braced himself.

'Give it to me.'

'Yes, sir.'

The note was simple and to the point. Marc stood immobile and read it while Dominic looked on.

Dear Marc

I never should have come. When you told me my sister was dead all I could think of was Henry. I assumed he'd need me, and to be honest I needed him as well. Loneliness is like that. It gets you. And I didn't see how you could care for him. I listened to your words. Not your heart.

But I've known you longer now: Long enough to understand that you'll care for Henry so well I need never worry. Sure, it'd be better if he had both of us, but a split childhood isn't going to work. Not if that split means you don't commit to him.

Marc, I know this isn't any of my business, but it seems to me that you've been running scared ever since your mother died. You've been terrified of getting involved. Of loving. But you've fallen for Henry. I came here because I thought Henry would be alone, but by the time the plane landed in Broitenburg I knew you'd look after him and love him. And these last few days I've learned that you need him as much as he needs you. You need to let down the barriers, and caring for Henry will do just that.

Maybe I'm naïve, Marc, but you kissing me...it changes things. It means that I can't bear to be close to you. Loving you is stupid.

I'm stupid. I hate it, but this is the only solution.

I'm going home.

CHAPTER ELEVEN

IT WAS the longest month of his life.

For the first week Marc stayed at Renouys. He hired a nanny who lasted for two whole days—just long enough for Marc to realise he couldn't bear for Henry to be awake and in the care of a stranger. He tried desperately to stay in his study and work, but over and over he'd hear Henry sob in frustration and he didn't have a choice but to investigate.

Then Henry's little face, dull and indifferent in the care of the impeccably referenced and very nice nanny, would crease into laughter at the sight of him. He'd hold out his arms to Marc, and Marc would be hooked.

So the nanny left, smiling her appreciation at a parent who really cared.

After that Henry settled into a predictable schedule. He woke at dawn, played for a couple of hours, slept mid-morning, played again, napped in the afternoon and slept solidly from about seven at night.

So for Marc it was easy. Almost. It was just a matter of fitting his work around Henry's schedule.

It didn't include a social life, but curiously he didn't seem to want one. The thought of the high life his friends were leading without him left him cold.

But staying in his wonderful château for the rest of his life while he cared for Henry wasn't so appealing either.

So what was it that he wanted?

Tammy.

He wanted her to come back, he thought over and over again, as the time she'd been away grew longer. He wanted her to return and take over Henry so he could get his life back again.

But…he didn't want his life. He'd just told himself he no longer missed the social hubbub he'd existed in before. Ingrid made a few interested phone calls—testing the water, but the water was ice-cold.

So he worked, he played with Henry, and he bonded to his small cousin as he'd never imagined he could bond in his life.

And he thought about Tammy.

She had to come back.

She wouldn't. He knew that about her now. She'd made her decision and she'd stick to it. Maybe if he mistreated his little cousin she'd return and whisk him back to Australia. Mistreating Henry wasn't an option, but that was the only way he'd get her back.

'So what will we do?' he asked Henry, and Henry gazed back at him and chortled as if extremely amused by the whole situation.

Great!

There were no answers. He could only take one step at a time—settle back at Renouys and wait.

And even that wasn't easy. The pressure was on for him to return to the palace.

'You should be here,' Dominic told him when he phoned to see how the staff were getting on. 'You know the whole of Broitenburg wants the royal family to live in residence. You're the state figurehead. You should be here.'

'Henry's the state figurehead,' Marc growled. 'And he's too young to live in that damned pile by himself.'

'You're the Prince Regent,' Dominic reminded him. 'Like it or not, you're the person everyone wants to see here. The people want you settled, with a family, in the palace where you belong.'

'I'm settled with Henry right here.'

'That's not what I meant.'

'You know damned well that I have no intention of getting married. Or living in that royal rabbit warren...'

'Whatever you say, sir,' Dominic said gently—and he set down the phone before Marc could say a word.

He was going crazy. Another week went past and then another. The press were screaming for a photo-shoot in the grounds of the palace—Henry back where he belonged. Marc delayed it for as long as he could, but finally had to concede. So they stood in the Broitenburg palace gardens while Henry beamed at every photographer as if he was a personal friend. He chortled and chuckled, he offered his teddy for photographers to inspect, and generally behaved as if he was born to stand in the front of the camera.

'Can we pop him down on the grass and let him crawl?' one of the photographers asked, and Marc obliged. But Henry was intent on practising his new skill, which was hauling himself to his feet and standing upright unsteadily by Marc's side. He could just balance...

'He could so easily be your son,' one of the photographers said, wondering at the look on Marc's face. 'You look like you love him.'

'He's a great kid,' Marc told them, unable to keep the pride from his face, and the photographers snapped on, entranced.

'We hear you're making the association official?'

'I'm hoping to eventually adopt him, yes.'

'All we need here is a mother...' one of the journalists said softly, and Marc's lips tightened. And then he felt the pressure ease from his leg. He looked down, expecting to see Henry plump down onto his bottom.

But Henry did no such thing. He'd released Marc's trouser leg and was intent on the next step, but first he had to check he had an audience. This was a baby with style!

He gazed up into his cousin's face—he gave him a huge grin—and took the very first tottering step of his life. He stepped. He balanced for an interminable moment while the Broitenburg press corps held its collective breath. Then he took one more step for effect before he sat down bump on the grass, deeply satisfied with what he'd achieved.

It was such a moment! Journalists and photographers were cheering and laughing, and Marc was staring down at his tiny charge in stupefaction. Such magic!

She should have been here to share it, he thought savagely, the knowledge of what she was missing hitting him like a thunderbolt. And the knowledge of what she'd given him.

She'd given him this. Tammy knew the joy such a moment would bring and she'd walked away. *She'd given it to him.*

The sensation was almost overwhelming. He hadn't seen it until now. He'd been a blind, stupid fool.

She hadn't wanted to go. Of course she hadn't. She'd brought up Lara almost by herself. She knew the hurt such loving could bring but she'd also known the joy. She'd known that in time he'd feel like this—so proud he could burst.

It was a gift that was so precious it took his breath away. Up until now he'd sworn not to love, but he hadn't known what he was doing. He hadn't known what love was.

Tammy had known—and what deeper love to have her walk away—gifting love to him?

Tammy…

'Tammy?'
'Mother?'

Tammy had been back in Australia for more than a month. An interminable time. Broitenburg was half a world away. She was back sleeping under the stars as she worked again in the wilderness, and the call on her cellphone late at night made her feel more confused than ever.

'I need to speak to you.' Her mother's voice was harsh and angry and Tammy came instantly awake.

'Is something wrong?'

It's Henry, she thought. There hadn't been a minute since she'd left that she hadn't thought about Henry—or his big dark cousin.

She'd heard nothing. The temptation to contact Dominic or Mrs Burchett had been almost irresistible, but she meant to continue as she'd started.

She'd trust Henry with Marc. She must.

So why was her mother ringing?

'Do you know the trouble I had to get your phone number?' her mother was demanding, and Tammy thought about it. That question, at least, was easy.

'No,' Tammy said bleakly. 'I don't. I gave this number to you years ago and you've never rung until now. Even when Lara died you didn't use it.'

'So I lost it,' her mother snapped. 'But now...'

'Now?' A cold dread was creeping round her heart. Had something happened? If something happened to Henry they'd probably contact her mother. Marc would contact her mother. Of course he would.

Why should he contact her?

'Have you seen the papers?'

The dread deepened. 'What papers?' Tammy flicked on her torch and checked her watch. Eleven p.m. Not so late then—for her mother. It was only to the likes of Tammy who rose at dawn that eleven o'clock seemed late.

'He's planning on adopting Henry.'

'Who...?'

'That Prince Marc.' Her mother's voice was practically vitriolic. 'He's wants to adopt Henry without even a by your leave. I'm the child's grandmother. It's plastered all over the *News of the World—Eligible playboy planning to adopt Heir to Throne*. There's even a picture of him, looking for all the world as if he cares.'

'And does he?' A rush of pure pleasure surged through Tammy's body and she felt herself grinning like a fool. *Looking for all the world as if he cares...*

'Who the hell knows if he cares or not? That's not the point. I've had journalists here trying to get a comment. A *comment*. From me! I tell you, Tammy, I want more than a damned comment. I rang a lawyer here and he says there's nothing I can do, but there has to be something. I mean, if he wants the kid so much there should be a payment of some sort. Anyway, the lawyer says you're his legal guardian. If he wants to adopt he'll have to send you papers to sign. So you can...'

'I can what?'

'Demand your rights.'

Tammy thought about it, trying to see where her mother was coming from. And she knew. Of course she knew. 'You mean money?'

'Of course I mean money.'

'There are other rights besides money,' she said slowly, switching off her torch and settling back into the dark while she let her mother's words sink in. 'Yes, I have rights to Henry, but I gave them to Marc willingly. I don't...I don't want them back.'

There was an indrawn breath and then a long silence. Communication between mother and daughter had always been thus. Tammy knew exactly what her mother wanted, and by now Isobelle knew exactly what her daughter's reply would be.

'You're a fool,' Isobelle said at last, and Tammy nodded into the dark.

'Maybe. It's what you've always called me.'

'If you'd played your cards right...'

'I could have stayed at the palace in Broitenburg and done nothing at all for the rest of my life.' While I loved Marc hopelessly from the sidelines, she added silently to herself. There was no way her mother would hear that. It was a comment for Tammy's heart alone.

'This is a waste of time. You deserve to die a spinster with your blasted trees,' her mother hissed, and Tammy ended the conversation without saying another word.

But she couldn't go back to sleep.

After a while she rose and climbed into her little truck and drove the half-hour into town to the all-night service station. There on the magazine rack was what she was searching for—the latest edition of the *News of the World*. She bought herself a coffee and took herself out to the cab of her truck to read it.

It was after midnight now. Apart from the gangly youth holding up the counter in the service station, no one was awake but her. The coffee was warm between her hands, but she found herself shivering as she turned the pages.

And there they were, splashed across page three. It was a lovely, lovely photograph of Marc holding a laughing Henry. The pair looked supremely happy with each other. They looked…at peace.

'I've done the right thing by both of them. I have.' But she found she was crying, tears slipping helplessly down her face while she stared sightlessly at the photograph and thought of what she'd thrown away.

But she hadn't thrown it away. What she so desperately wanted had never been offered. What had been offered was a series of one-day access to Henry followed by one day of isolation. It would have been a disrupted upbringing for Henry—and Marc didn't come into the equation at all.

Or complete isolation. Sole guardianship of Henry with Marc not coming close.

'At least this way Henry's safe. And Marc...he's softened. He'll love him to bits.'

Her coffee was growing cold but she stared on, thinking of the lonely little tent waiting for her back in the clearing. She'd made her choice. It was the right choice—but she'd never felt so lonely in all her life.

Marc...

Tammy was up a tree when royalty arrived.

It wasn't the same tree as the last time Marc had arrived, but it might have been. She was thirty feet up a magnificent eucalypt, and she might as well have been alone in the world. There was Tammy and her tree and no one else.

Or that was what she thought. In reality Doug, the team foreman, was straight underneath her, pointing upward, and beside him were Marc and Henry.

'Hey, Tam. You've got visitors,' Doug called, and then grinned and took his departure. He suspected he might be losing his very favourite worker, but Tammy hadn't been the same since she'd returned from her overseas jaunt. She usually sang as she worked, but she'd returned from Broitenburg pale-faced and silent. Doug had employed enough young men and women in his time to know there was probably a love affair behind this, and by the look on this particular man's face as he'd asked for directions he might just be the cause.

So he had directed Marc to the clearing and then pointed upward. And left them to it.

'Hi,' Marc said as Tammy stared stupidly down. She was swinging in her harness but her world was spinning far, far faster.

'H...hi,' she said at last, and her voice cracked a little. 'What are you doing here?'

'Looking for you.'

'You've found me.'

'So I have,' Marc said carefully, and then he set Henry carefully on his feet. The clearing was covered with soft moss and undergrowth; it was a glorious place for a little boy to explore and Henry had been buckled into his baby seat for far too long. 'I need to speak to your aunt,' Marc told the little boy. 'So if you'll excuse me for a minute…?'

And he leapt up to catch a lower limb and started to climb.

Which left Tammy breathless with shock. 'You haven't got a harness,' she managed, and Marc grinned.

'Neither I have.' Tammy's voice had been a squeak of alarm but Marc's was rock-steady.

'You'll fall.'

'I've fallen.'

'I don't…' She was breathing way, way too fast. It was such a shock—seeing him. This was a very different Marc from the one she'd seen first. He was wearing casual jeans and a faded sweater—gear more suitable for climbing trees than for being Prince Regent of Broitenburg—but he was still Marc for all that.

He was still capable of taking her breath away.

'I don't know what you mean,' she said at last. He was twenty feet up and climbing as surely as if he'd spent his life in trees. 'You've fallen where?'

'I've fallen for you.'

That was another breath-taker. She had some serious thinking to do here, but her thinking mechanisms seemed all upside down. Below them Henry was watching in wide-eyed wonder. His cousin climbing trees was something new.

'You should be in Broitenburg,' Tammy managed. 'Aren't you risking Henry's ascendancy or something? Bringing him here?'

'Henry's ascendancy no longer matters.'

'I don't know what you mean,' she repeated. She suc-ceeded in sounding cross this time and his grin widened, despite the problems he was having in the climbing department. She really was too far up for comfort. He was making this climbing business look easy, but he really should have a harness and he had to take care. He hadn't come this far to break his neck.

At least not before he kissed her.

At least not before he claimed her.

'I'm officially adopting Henry,' he told her as he tried to focus on staying in the tree. 'If you agree. I have the papers in the car. That means Henry gets to inherit regardless. If he stays out of the country for longer than specified then he loses out on being first in line to the throne, but if he's officially my son then he gets to be second in line after I inherit.'

'Which means he inherits if you fall on your head,' she managed. 'Marc, be careful. You need a harness to be safe.'

'I don't need anything of the sort.' He'd reached her now, hauling himself up onto the wide branch she'd tied herself to. She was swinging beside him in her sling-seat and he caught her and pulled her into him. The motion made him wobble, and she had to put out her hands to catch him and steady him. And hold…

'Hey.' He held her right back, and it was just as well she was wearing a harness as it meant that at least one of them was anchored to the tree. And if one of them was anchored then both of them were, because neither was letting go.

'Tammy.' His face was two inches from hers and he was smiling into her eyes with such a look…

She stopped breathing altogether at that. After all, why should she breathe? There were much more interesting things to do in life than breathe.

'Have you missed me?' he asked, and she just gazed at him with a look that meant it was his turn to stop breathing. Stupid question, her look said. Yeah, it was definitely a stupid question.

He hadn't realised she was this beautiful, he decided. He'd imagined her all the time she was away, and his imagination had said she was the most gorgeous woman in the world. His imagination had underestimated it. Her eyes were melting into him. She was small and waif-like, but warm and rounded and tanned and lovely. Now her wide eyes were filled with confusion, but filled with something else as well.

His Tammy.

'I...did you come to get the adoption papers signed?'

'No.'

'Then why...?'

'Because I didn't see,' he murmured and her hands held him in tighter. She was just stopping him from falling. She was just stopping herself from falling.

They were stopping each other from falling—but they were both falling so fast the world was whizzing past them.

The world didn't matter.

'You didn't see...what?' she whispered, and he held her tighter.

'How much you were giving.'

'I don't understand.'

'Neither did I.' He was holding her strongly now, regardless of the fact that they were sitting on a branch thirty feet in the air. He was holding her as if he was holding the woman he loved rather than the woman who would keep them both safe through her harness.

Maybe it was the same thing. Maybe this was the woman who would keep him safe for ever.

'I fell in love with Henry,' he told her.

She was so confused she didn't have a clue what was happening, but her heart was beginning to sing. Joy. Oh, joy... 'Of course you did.'

'But I hadn't realised,' Marc said seriously. He put her away from him then—just a little—so he could gaze into those wonderful eyes and make her see. 'You fell for Henry the first time you met him. Because you knew what love was.'

'Yes, but...'

'But you let him go,' he said. 'You let him go so he'd love me. So that I'd know what love was. So I'd lose this crazy shield I'd built up. You didn't run away from responsibility. You gave away the most precious thing in the world. You gave me love.'

'I...'

'It was a gift without price,' he said, and the smile behind his eyes was such that she stopped breathing all over again. 'I hadn't seen it. And then Henry took his first steps.'

'Henry's *walking*?'

'He sure is.' They both looked down to where Henry was taking teetering steps on the mossy forest floor. 'I was there to see it. So was half the press corps of Broitenburg. But you weren't. You'd left. You'd given me love and then you'd left. And you should have been there. You should be there.'

'Marc, I c...can't...' she stammered, and he put his finger on her lips and shook his head.

'You can't do what I asked you? No. I won't accept taking Henry every second day and you can't take full responsibility for him. Because that way I'd be the loser. Only I didn't see it until now. So I'm not here to relinquish responsibility, Tammy. For anything.'

'I don't...' She couldn't go on. She was so confused she was speechless.

But Marc knew what he had to say and he said it.

'I'm taking responsibility for my country,' he told her seriously—because this had to be said. It had to be cleared between them. She had to know what she was getting into. If she'd take the next step... 'When Jean-Paul died I was appalled. I wasn't stepping into his shoes because I couldn't accept the role of royalty. I thought royalty was a goldfish bowl and there was nothing in it for me. But I've learned to see. Sure it's a goldfish bowl; sure, it's a huge load of responsibility but it means I can take control of my country's future. I can care for my people. I can care for you.'

He pressed his fingers on her wondering lips and he smiled—such a smile!

'When I first met you I was desperate to offload that responsibility,' he told her. 'I wanted Henry to have it regardless. I'd have put Henry into the care of nannies, I'd have done what I had to to keep him materially cared for and I'd have kept my distance. But now…thanks to you…'

'I haven't done anything.'

'Oh, but you have.' The tenderness in his eyes was all-enveloping. 'You look at me just as you're looking at me now. You trust me as you trusted me when you walked away and left me with Henry. You love…'

'I can't…'

'You can't love me?' The smile died a little and his brow furrowed. 'Tammy, you must. You must. You see, I love you so much. If I've killed it… Tell me I haven't killed it. Tell me I can't have been that stupid.' His hands held hers, urgently pleading. 'I want you, Tammy. I want you to be my wife. I want you and me to return to Broitenburg in all honour—husband and wife with our son between us, ready to accept the crown and all it entails. Ready to take on the joys and the sorrows of our country. Ready to take on the joys and sorrows of our family.

'But mostly…' His voice softened and there was a look of such uncertainty in his eyes that Tammy felt her heart twist within her. 'Mostly joy. Tammy, if you'll marry me— if you'll love me for ever… I can't imagine any greater joy than that. Will you marry me, my heart? Will you be Crown Princess of Broitenburg, mother to Henry—wife to me? Will you be my love—now and for ever?'

And what was a girl to say to that?

Tammy Dexter, tree surgeon extraordinaire—clad in overalls with her hair braided down her back, with a smut on the end of her nose and with tears in her eyes—Tammy Dexter looked long and deeply into the eyes of the man she loved with all her heart.

Crown Prince of Broitenburg?

No.

He was her Marc.

'Of course I'll marry you,' she whispered. 'Oh, my love, how can you doubt it? Of course I'll marry you.'

'You will?'

He hadn't been sure. She could see it in his eyes—in the exultant joy that flashed across his face and in the way he fumbled uncertainly in the pocket of his jeans. He hadn't thought she would.

He was smiling and smiling—their eyes locked as he fumbled for the blasted box—and then he swore as the tiny crimson box came too fast out of its hiding place. The lid came up; Tammy saw a flash of diamonds and then watched as a tiny sparkling ring tumbled downward to the leaf litter below.

Henry saw it fall. He watched as this bright sparkling thing landed at his feet and he gave it his very serious attention. Slowly he bent and lifted it to inspect it from all angles.

'We'd better go down,' Tammy said—very, very unsteadily. How could her voice be anything but unsteady through tears? 'If my nephew's holding what I think he's holding.'

'He's holding our future,' Marc told her. His hands caught her to him and he kissed her—a kiss of love and wonder and promise of joy to come. 'He's holding our future in his hands.'

'Then we'd better go down fast,' Tammy said between laughter and tears and pure, bright joy. 'We'd better descend right now, before the heir apparent to the throne of Broitenburg decides he might eat it.'

'It's a letter from Tammy.'

It was teabreak for Doug and the team. The billy was steaming on the campfire and Tammy's old foreman had ripped open the letter with the royal insignia and was planning to read it to the three team members clustered around. 'Will you listen to this?'

He read.

> *Dear Doug, Lucy, Danny and Mia*
>
> *Thank you so much for your letter. This is such a wonderful place that I hardly have time to be homesick, but I do miss you.*
>
> *We've been so busy. Marc has taken on the role of Crown Prince, with all the responsibility that entails. We've officially adopted our beloved Henry, so one day he'll inherit the throne—as he should—but this way responsibility comes as it would if his father had survived. We figure this way he's going to have a much more carefree childhood, with the attention taken from him. It's the right decision. Henry's happy as a piglet in mud, as are we all.*
>
> *The reason I'm writing now is to ask for your help. The woodland here needs serious work. Otto, our head gardener, and I have been trying to treat the trees, but the woodland was planted three hundred years ago. We need manpower, and Marc and I were wondering whether the four of you would like to take a couple of months' break from Australian natives and help us out.*
>
> *There's a lot I can do myself, but Marc is being funny about me abseiling right now. I guess he'll be like that for the next few months. Can you imagine why? I admit my bump will get in the way a bit, but we're so excited*

it's worth it. Marc can't keep the grin from his face. He
walks around the palace smiling and smiling—almost as
much as I am.

Well. Enough of bumps and babies and soppy romance
with happy endings. We'd like you to do the work so you
have first offer. Can we send you plane fares?

Will you come?

Doug set down the letter and picked up the magazine
Lucy was holding out to him. Lucy was a damned fine tree
surgeon but she wasn't a patch on Tammy. Could he take
the team to this odd place called Broitenburg?

'It's too darned foreign. I bet they don't have meat pies
and tomato sauce,' he said doubtfully. 'They'd probably try
and make us eat truffles.'

'I've always wanted to try truffles,' Lucy said. 'And…it
looks great.'

'Yeah?'

'Yeah.' Lucy had the magazine opened to the centrefold,
and she pointed. 'Look.'

Doug looked down at the photograph. It had been taken
six months ago, on Tammy's wedding day.

There they were. Marc and Tammy. Bride and groom. He
was in his full royal regalia, sword by his side, stunningly
handsome. She was all in white—a fairy princess. But,
amazing as the wonderful clothes were, the focus was their
faces.

The love in their eyes shone out for the whole world to
see. Here was a true prince with his princess. Marc with his
Tammy.

There was an elderly gentleman standing beside
them—'Dominic, Head Steward of the household', the blurb
said. He was holding a little boy with all the pride of a
grandpa. Behind them were the castle staff, and there was
joy on every single face.

In the background was the castle, glistening in its glory.

'It looks a happy place to be,' Lucy said, and her voice sounded wistful.

'Magic,' Danny agreed. Danny was almost seventy years old, and had never been out of Australia in his life. 'All them turrets and things. And look at Tammy in that glittery white dress with the veil and all. She looks like a real princess.'

'She *is* a princess,' Mia said, and they all laughed.

But there were serious issues at stake here. 'Tammy wants us to come,' Doug said as their laughter faded. And they all thought about it.

'There's nothing to say, then, is there?' Danny said at last into the stillness. 'She's the princess. What royalty commands, royalty gets. Let's go fix her trees.'

National Bestselling Author

brenda novak

COLD FEET

Despite the cloud of suspicion that followed her father to his
grave, Madison Lieberman maintained his innocence...*until* crime
writer Caleb Trovato forces her to confront the past once again.

**"Readers will quickly be drawn into this well-written,
multi-faceted story that is an engrossing, compelling read."**
—*Library Journal*

Available February 2004.

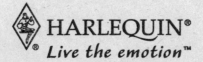

HARLEQUIN®
Live the emotion™

Visit us at www.eHarlequin.com

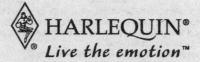

If you enjoyed what you just read,
then we've got an offer you can't resist!

Take 2 bestselling
love stories FREE!
Plus get a FREE surprise gift!

Clip this page and mail it to Harlequin Reader Service®

IN U.S.A.	IN CANADA
3010 Walden Ave.	P.O. Box 609
P.O. Box 1867	Fort Erie, Ontario
Buffalo, N.Y. 14240-1867	L2A 5X3

YES! Please send me 2 free Harlequin Romance® novels and my free surprise gift. After receiving them, if I don't wish to receive anymore, I can return the shipping statement marked cancel. If I don't cancel, I will receive 6 brand-new novels every month, before they're available in stores! In the U.S.A., bill me at the bargain price of $3.34 plus 25¢ shipping & handling per book and applicable sales tax, if any*. In Canada, bill me at the bargain price of $3.80 plus 25¢ shipping & handling per book and applicable taxes**. That's the complete price and a savings of 10% off the cover prices—what a great deal! I understand that accepting the 2 free books and gift places me under no obligation ever to buy any books. I can always return a shipment and cancel at any time. Even if I never buy another book from Harlequin, the 2 free books and gift are mine to keep forever.

186 HDN DNTX
386 HDN DNTY

Name	(PLEASE PRINT)	
Address	Apt.#	
City	State/Prov.	Zip/Postal Code

* Terms and prices subject to change without notice. Sales tax applicable in N.Y.
** Canadian residents will be charged applicable provincial taxes and GST.
All orders subject to approval. Offer limited to one per household and not valid to current Harlequin Romance® subscribers.
® are registered trademarks of Harlequin Enterprises Limited.

HROM02   ©2001 Harlequin Enterprises Limited